Hockeytown™ Hero:
The Steve Yzerman Story

An authorized biography
by
Shelley Lazarus

Cover design by Jeffrey Wisniewski

Proctor Publications, LLC • Ann Arbor • Michigan • USA

Library of Congress Catalog Number: 2001-131134

Publisher's Cataloging-in-Publication
(Provided by Quality Books, Inc.)

Lazarus, Shelley.
    Hockeytown hero : the Steve Yzerman story / by
Shelley Lazarus. -- 1st. ed.
    p. cm.
    Includes bibliographical references and index.
    ISBN: 1-928623-04-2

    1. Yzerman, Steve. 2. Hockey players--Canada--
Biography.   I. Title.

GV848.5.Y94L39 2001   796.962'092
                                 QBI01-200084

www.otterbooks.net

ii

This book is dedicated to:

Dad,
who taught me to write a business letter

Janie,
who taught me the game of hockey

and

Eric,
who gives me time and support.

Acknowledgments

This book would not have been possible without the help of many people.

First I want to thank Steve. He was generous with his time and was cooperative throughout the project. It's a pleasure to be associated with such a talented, gracious, and humble person.

Darren Pang, Dick Todd, Herb Warr, Cathie Webster, Tim Carmichael, Rick Bugnet, and Peter Peckett were all extremely helpful when I was working on the Nepean and Peterborough chapters of the book. They provided names, numbers, stats and quotes when I needed them most.

I now have a greater appreciation for hockey beat writers for the *Detroit Free Press*, *The Detroit News* and *The Oakland Press*. The game story chronology built by reporters like Viv Bernstein, Nicholas J. Cotsonika, Keith Gave, Ansar Kahn, Jason La Canfora, Cynthia Lambert, John Lowe, Bill McGraw, Drew Sharp, Helene St. James, and Charlie Vincent enabled me to accurately rebuild Steve's career from the moment he set foot in Detroit to the present. Their stories also brought back lots of memories for me as I did my research. Special thanks to Lynn Henning, Charles Robinson, Ted Kulfan, and Paula Pasche who helped me at practice.

I also wish to thank the Detroit Red Wings organization for their help. Jimmy Devellano, John Hahn, Mike Kuta, Scotty Bowman, Dave Lewis, Barry Smith, John Wharton and a number of Wings players were generous with their time and patient with my questions. Bill Jamieson, former Public Relations Director for the Wings, was also helpful and shared many great stories.

A special thank you to Bryan Trottier. Your comments exemplify the respect and admiration people in and out of hockey have for Steve, both on and off the ice.

Gene Myers, Mary Schroeder, Gina Brintley, Owen Davis, and Jenny Koss of the *Detroit Free Press* were exceptionally helpful with the photos. Ron and Jean Yzerman provided the photos of Steve when he was young.

Thanks to Denise, Janie, Brad Betker, Jo-Ann

Barnas and members of my writing group who read the manuscript and offered comments and suggestions.

I want to recognize Stewart Roberts and Phil Stamp of *The A to Z Encyclopedia of Ice Hockey* (see Resources) who let me use many of their definitions in the glossary. Laura Ramus was helpful with the medical definitions.

Finally, I want to thank the students of Pine Lake Elementary School. You had some great questions!

Table of Contents

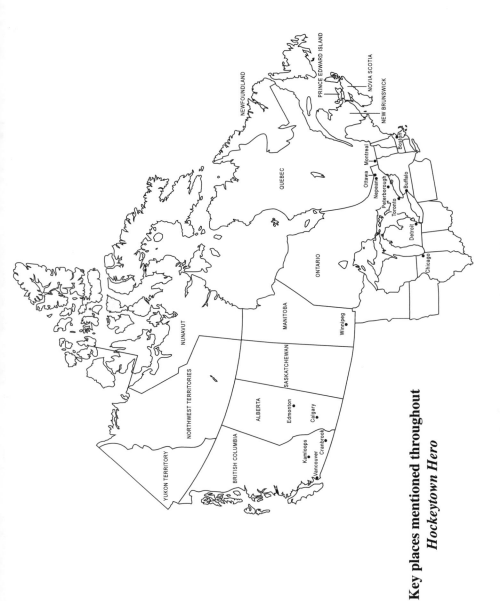

Key places mentioned throughout
Hockeytown Hero

The Stanley Cup. It had eluded Steve Yzerman for 13 years and the city of Detroit for 42. In 1997, all that changed. Now, for the second year in a row, Yzerman circled the ice, lifting hockey's prized possession high over his head. The Detroit Red Wings had just defeated the Washington Capitals 4-1, sweeping the series in four games as they had done the previous season against the Philadelphia Flyers. Moments earlier, Yzerman had raised the Conn Smythe Trophy recognizing him as the playoffs' Most Valuable Player. It was a night when Steve Yzerman finally got the credit and respect he deserved. It was a night every young, hockey-playing Canadian boy dreams of . . .

1

Everything Sports-Related

On a cold winter's day, Steve Yzerman, his older brother, Mike, and their parents headed to a frozen lake for a day of skating. Steve was about 3 years old and ready to take to the ice in a pair of **bobskates**. Although it would be another two years before he played organized hockey, it was the first step toward learning the skills that would make him a hockey superstar.

Steve was born to Ron and Jean Yzerman, May 9, 1965, in Cranbrook, British Columbia. As a young boy, Steve skated and watched a lot of hockey with his father. He remembers seeing the New York Rangers take on the Boston Bruins in one of the first professional hockey games they watched together on television. As Steve grew older, he began watching the Vancouver Canucks' games. The more he watched, the more he knew he wanted to play hockey.

Around this time, Mike started playing on an organized hockey team. After attending some of Mike's games, Steve asked his father if he could play too. Ron Yzerman told his son that, at age 4, he wasn't old enough yet. The following year, his father declared Steve was ready. Steve joined his first team and attended a hockey camp.

"I played as a 5-year-old but I couldn't skate," Steve says. "I could get up and fall down. Then I went to hockey camp that summer. That's where I learned how to skate and picked it up pretty quickly.

"My first year we played on a rink and they divided it into three. You played half across the ice. You had one game going in the end zone, one in the middle and one in the other end. We were 5-year-olds. We really couldn't stand up. That was great!"

His first goal was really nothing to be proud of.

"I had fallen down in front of the net," Steve told Bill McGraw, a *Detroit Free Press* reporter. "Their guy banked it off one of their guys' skates and into the net. I was lying there and I got credit for it."

2

Like most Canadian boys, Steve watched hockey, played on hockey teams, and dreamed of becoming a professional hockey player. He emulated his own hockey hero, the New York Islanders' Bryan Trottier. He admired the way Trottier conducted himself on the ice and saw him as a solid, all-around player. Steve also strived to be a great all-around player, imitating Trottier's every move, from the taping of his stick to the way he celebrated a goal.

But Steve didn't limit himself to hockey. He enjoyed a variety of sports and played them any time he got the chance. He sought out a neighborhood game as quickly as he did an organized match.

"I was into all sports," Steve says. "In the summer, we played hockey. We played street hockey. We played grass hockey. As a kid, it was sports and whatever game was going on, we were playing it."

Being such an avid sports fan, Steve did more than just watch and play. He admits sports were involved in every facet of his life. When Steve picked up a book, it was almost always one about a favorite athlete.

"I used to read biographies," Steve says. "I read about Bobby Orr. I read about Joe Namath, Fran Tarkenton and Kareem Abdul-Jabbar. Pretty much everything I did was sports-related."

But not all his sports-related activities were so serious. Steve and his brothers were also hockey card collectors. However, these cards didn't get the special treatment many collectors give their cards today.

"Yeah, we collected cards," says Steve, thinking back. "I had three brothers, so the four of us had stacks and stacks of them. What we used to do is play a game where you'd line them up on the wall, then flick them and try to knock over the other cards. That's what we did with them! We would all collect them, keep cards of all the players, and look at them. But we played games with them. When we were teenagers and we were all starting to move out of the house, we probably had a fortune's worth of old hockey cards, but my mom just threw them out. Collecting wasn't the big deal it is now."

Steve lived in Cranbrook until he was 7 years old. Living in another part of British Columbia for a couple of years, Steve took advantage of the rugged land that surrounded him. He expanded his sports repertoire to include hiking.

In 1973, when Steve was 8, he played for the Moose Pup All-Stars in Kamloops, British Columbia. This was one of his first travel teams. Steve's brother Mike also played for the team. Steve is in the front row, third from the right and Mike is next to him, second from right.

"We lived in a city called Kamloops for two years," he recalls. "It was a fun place to play. We lived on a street that was kind of the last street in the town and behind us were the hills. All summer, we spent our whole day hiking up in those hills. You could literally go forever. That was a fun place to live because there were a lot of outdoor things to do. When I played in Kamloops, actually, [hockey] became more competitive and we traveled around to local cities. As a 10-year-old, we moved to Ottawa and that's where I started playing soccer in the summer."

Although he had the company of his brothers and sister, he was also glad he played sports. It kept him busy and it helped him make friends in his new hometown.

"That definitely made it a lot easier," says Steve. "It was the easiest way to meet other kids and make friends. Playing on the hockey team kept me busy after school."

It was in Nepean, a suburb of Ottawa, Ontario, that Steve's hockey playing steadily increased. He was no longer playing in the **house leagues**.

"There are different levels," Steve says. "There's A, B and C and a lot of kids play. The A league, you do a lot more traveling. The B team is kids who didn't make the A team. Then after that it would basically just be local leagues, just in the area. They don't have to travel all over."

Steve had reached the level of play required to earn a position on a travel team. He was on the ice for practices and games as many as five days a week. He participated in tournaments. At 14, Steve was playing Junior A Tier 2 hockey in the Central Junior Hockey League (**CJHL**) with the Nepean Raiders. His parents, supportive of his hockey playing, took Steve wherever he needed to go.

In 1977, Steve's Pee Wee team won the Ontario Provincial Championship. Steve is in the front row, third from the right.

"My brother and I played a lot of hockey and my parents were constantly driving us around," Steve says. "We both played in a lot of tournaments where, from Ottawa, we'd drive to Toronto, all over Ontario, into Quebec, and occasionally down into the States. It was a big commitment for my parents and a real sacrifice for my sister and my two younger brothers. My parents were spending a lot of time during the hockey season with us."

Some of Steve's best memories of playing hockey as a youth come from his days in Nepean. When he played peewee hockey at age 12, Steve's team won the Ontario Provincial Championship. Later, when playing for the Raiders in 1980-81, Steve had one of his most memorable seasons.

"I played in that league as a 15-year-old and it was one of my most enjoyable years," Steve says. "We had a good team. That's when I became friends with Darren Pang. I played with a really good bunch of guys. I was 15 and playing with guys up to 20 years old. It was one of the most enjoyable years I'd had in hockey."

Steve contributed 38 goals and 54 assists to help the Raiders finish first in the regular season. Although Steve added four goals and 11 assists in the playoffs, the Raiders lost to the Gloucester Rangers in the finals. Steve left the league banquet with two trophies, Rookie of the Year and Outstanding Midget in the League, and the honor of being named the league's first-team All-Star center.

Pang remembers that, even at 15, Steve had incredible talent.

"It was very obvious," says Pang, a former goalie and now an announcer for ESPN. "Not only the fact that he was a real special individual player, I always thought that he was light years ahead of everybody else in terms of maturity. He always kind of kept himself on a nice even keel and then, when he got onto the ice, he did such special things with the puck."

He also remembers how Steve could spark the team.

"Whenever you were down a goal and you needed something special to happen," says Pang "he would literally put the team on his back and make something happen. You know, players like that, when they come around and you get a chance to play with them… I mean… nothing's for sure in life but you look and say, 'Oh boy, this guy's going to be a good one, if not a great one.' He's turned out to be a great one."

It was during this time that Steve began to think he might have a future playing hockey. When Steve was 14, the Raiders put him on a **protected list**, just like those used in the National Hockey League (**NHL**) drafts. This meant no other team could draft Steve to play for it. He was assured a spot on the Raiders' roster the following season.

"I started taking it seriously," Steve says. "That's when the junior team scouts started coming to watch the games."

In two years, Steve would find out how serious the scouts really were.

2

The Peterborough Years

At 16, most kids are in the middle of high school. They are hanging out with their friends, doing their homework and always have home as a haven. But this age brought a much different life for Steve. He moved up to Major Junior Hockey, drafted by the Peterborough Petes of the Ontario Hockey League. With 160 miles between Nepean and Peterborough, Steve had to make a move. In order to play for the Petes, he and teammate Mike Posavad would leave home and take up residence with Vince and Lottie Garvey. The Garveys lived two blocks from the arena and provided accommodations for a number of Peterborough players through the years. Steve remembers them fondly.

"A majority of the junior teams are supported really well through the community," says Steve. "Families volunteer to take in players. The team pays room and board. I was with an unbelievable family. They were an older couple. Their children were grown and they were big hockey fans. The Garveys were great people. [They] spoiled us rotten!"

Peterborough drafted Steve, impressed with the offensive ability he demonstrated in Nepean. Early in his career with the Petes, other strengths in his game emerged. Former Petes coach Dick Todd recalls that Steve didn't have many glaring weaknesses, even at 16.

"Steve came to us very young and very small, but he had tremendous offensive skills," remembers Todd. "Coming in to Peterborough, he was

At 16, Steve was drafted by the Peterborough Petes of the Ontario Hockey League.

already very offensive-minded. If anything, we didn't have the toughness on the team to protect him. But Steve also had the ability to learn. He became a well-rounded player."

Todd also remembers Steve's unselfishness when it came to helping teammates score. One of the Petes' leading scorers was Bob Errey. One reason for that was Steve's play.

"Another thing Steve could do was draw the defense to him and pass off to Bob," Todd says. "Steve did all right when it came to scoring goals. He had between 40 and 50 his second year. But Bob's production was higher because Steve was able to get him open."

While playing for the Petes, team members were also required to attend school or work at a job. Expectations for players off the ice were just as high as when they were playing. Parents received progress reports monthly. If players were having difficulty with school, the team provided tutors. Steve attended Thomas A. Stewart Collegiate his two years in Peterborough. Todd remembers Steve handled school with the same confidence and finesse as hockey.

Todd, now a scout with the New York Rangers, was a medical and equipment trainer with the Petes when Steve started in 1981-82. Dave Dryden was head coach. That December, when team members had differences with Dryden's coaching style, Dryden left. Todd took over as head coach. He coached the remainder of Steve's two-year career with the Petes. Steve credits Dryden and Todd with teaching him important aspects of his game.

"It was beneficial for me," Steve says, "because it was a team where the two coaches that I played for spent a lot of time teaching me how to play away from the puck, meaning playing your position defensively. That was the first time I'd ever spent time, in practice or talking before the games, playing defensively. [They taught us] who to pick up **back-checking** and, in your own zone, what your responsibility was. Before that, when you practiced and played, you basically tried to make a play to score a goal. You didn't really work on the defensive part of the game. Going there was the first time

I spent any time on it. They stressed it there."

To this day, Todd remains one of Steve's favorite and most influential coaches.

"I really enjoyed playing for Dick Todd," says Steve. "He taught you a lot about the game and he was a really honest man. He'd tell you about the way you played. If he didn't like what you were doing or he was saying something to help you, he would just say it honestly, plain as day. Whatever it was, he wouldn't pull any punches. I really liked him for that. I was comfortable around him."

Todd, unlike other junior coaches, was known for playing all four lines consistently every game. He didn't give star players large amounts of ice time. Some coaches and players criticized this. They felt this philosophy hurt players' statistics and didn't allow standout players a chance to be recognized by pro scouts. However, Todd saw it differently. He felt this system gave every player a chance to contribute to the team's success. It also meant he wasn't rebuilding the team each year when he lost graduating players.

This system gave Steve somewhat average statistics for his two years in Peterborough. It also gave him something much more valuable: the concept that if he would play offense and defense with equal energy, the team could achieve larger goals. That would later enable Steve to adapt to coach Scotty Bowman's style in Detroit. Peterborough also gave Steve another opportunity that enhanced his hockey career: international competition.

"We had a pretty good team, but both years we lost in the second round of the playoffs," Steve remembers. "I learned a lot from playing there. I got to play in the World Junior Championships my second year in Peterborough, over in the Soviet Union. It was a great experience. We got the bronze medal."

When Steve left Peterborough, he knew he had a strong rating for the 1983 **NHL Entry Draft**. His second year at Peterborough, Steve's statistics were solid: 42 goals and 49 assists for a total of 91 points. He carved out a role as a play-making center with strong goal-scoring skills. He played under a coach whose philosophy focused on team effort and playing both ends of the rink. All this experience came together to make one nice package for some lucky NHL team. The question was: which one?

3

The Winged Wheel

Montreal was the site of the 1983 NHL Entry Draft. Steve was rated by NHL scouts as the fourth pick overall. He was aware that at least two teams were looking at him as a possible draft pick. Jimmy Devellano, general manager for the Detroit Red Wings, brought Steve to Detroit for a visit and let him know they were interested in him.

"He pretty much did most things well for a player of his age," Devellano remembers. "Certainly he could skate. He had good hockey sense. He could handle the puck. He was able to score and make plays. That's about all you want in a hockey player! And he was able to do those things above average for a kid his age."

But Devellano did not want to give Steve false hope. He told Steve he was looking to pick the highest-rated player available when his turn came. There was a good chance that could be Waterford, Michigan, native Pat LaFontaine, who was rated third.

"Certainly I was up front with Steve," says Devellano, now senior vice-president with the Wings. "You were dealing with two pretty good hockey players – Pat LaFontaine and Yzerman – probably fairly equal and both were 18. The advantage one had was he was Detroit born and bred. Obviously, that was an important consideration because in 1983, Detroit wasn't 'Hockeytown.' The building was three-quarters empty and selling tickets was very, very important."

Bill Torrey, general manager for the New York Islanders, had spoken with Steve on the phone. He also expressed an interest in Steve's talent. With his high rating, it looked certain he would be chosen early. He just didn't know by which team.

Steve didn't have a preference. He was just hoping to get picked. He thought about the chance to play for the Islanders. It was one of his favorite teams anchored by his favorite player, Bryan Trottier. But the Islanders also had won four consecutive Stanley Cups. Steve knew it would be difficult earning a position on a team full of such great talent.

Detroit, on the other hand, was in the process of rebuilding its team. Over the previous 17 seasons, the Red Wings made the playoffs only twice. Mike and Marian Ilitch of Little Caesars Pizza had purchased the team the previous summer. Devellano, the new general manager, had been the Islanders' chief scout for their first three Stanley Cup teams. He was hoping to work the same magic in Detroit. He wanted to start rebuilding the franchise with his first draft pick. Steve might earn a spot on the roster, but he would be playing for a struggling team.

"For me, getting drafted in Detroit was ideal because new management had taken over the year before and they really didn't have a lot of players under contract," Steve says. "They needed players. If I could keep up and I could play, I would have a job. I had a job to win or lose on my own. I was able to show that I could play at this level. It worked out well and I played regularly from the first game. For a young player, that's the

A familiar sight to Wings fans – Steve celebrates another goal.

ideal situation."

Bill Jamieson, director of public relations for the
Wings from 1982-96, remembers this draft was important for Detroit. The Wings' fans were excited. It seemed
everything businessman Mike Ilitch did was successful. They hoped he would have the same success with
the floundering Wings.

"It was a big deal," says Jamieson. "It was the first
draft of the Ilitch era. Anything Mr. Ilitch had been involved with, he'd had a real Midas touch. There was
that same attitude toward the Red Wings. Now that Mike
Ilitch owned the team, things were going to be better."

The day of the draft was exciting. Steve was nervous but, thanks to his high rating, he did not have to
wait long to know his fate. The Minnesota North Stars
nabbed Brian Lawton with the number one pick. Sylvain
Turgeon, at number two, went to the Hartford Whalers.
The New York Islanders drafted LaFontaine third. Moments later, Steve found out he would wear the winged
wheel on his jersey, representing the Detroit Red Wings.
He remembers the draft went quickly.

"It was a real whirlwind day," Steve says. "You get there and the draft starts. You're nervous. It's less pomp and circumstance than it is today. The guy steps up to the microphone and reads off the names and you go to the table. The Islanders picked third and chose Pat LaFontaine. I was picked by Detroit and went."

At Detroit's table, Steve met Mike and Marian Ilitch, Devellano, Jamieson, coach Nick Polano and some of the Detroit scouts. Jamieson whisked Steve off to do interviews by phone with the Detroit newspapers. It was the first of many times Steve would demonstrate his confidence and maturity for the Detroit media.

"He handled it well," remembers Jamieson. "He was just himself. He was very unpretentious."

Detroit started the 1983-84 season with high hopes. Prior to this, fans referred to the team as the "Dead Things." Since the mid-'60s, the Wings had managed to make the playoffs only twice, never going beyond the early rounds. Attendance was down. Consistent goal-scorers were nonexistent. That was about to change.

Steve made his NHL debut October 5, 1983, in a

road game against the Winnipeg Jets. He gave the Wings a quick return on their investment by scoring a goal and adding an assist. Still, the outcome was not in the Wings' favor. Detroit was leading 6-5 with only four minutes left in the game. Suddenly, the Jets' Doug Smail blazed in and put the puck past Wings goalie Eddie Mio. The game ended in a 6-6 tie, but Detroit's coaches saw what they wanted to see: a composed **rookie** who was ready to take on the NHL. In Bill McGraw's game story for the *Detroit Free Press* the next day, Coach Polano gave Steve high marks.

"He always looked dangerous," Polano said. "That tells you something, especially on the road. This was a good test for Steve. He showed he's ready to play."

Steve continued to show he was ready to play. In a 9-2 victory over the Toronto Maple Leafs on December 23, 1983, Steve got his first **hat trick**. He added an assist as the Wings ended an 11-game winless streak. For the rest of the season, Steve made a difference.

He posted 39 goals and 48 assists for a total of 87 points. This set team records for goals and points by a rookie. He was named top rookie by *The Sporting News* and voted to the NHL All-Rookie Team. Steve was runner-up in the voting for the Calder Trophy, which recognizes the NHL's Rookie of the Year. The Wings, who had been denied post-season play the previous five years, finished third and earned a playoff spot. In 1984, Steve was also picked to represent his country in the Canada Cup tournament. He returned to the Wings' training camp that fall with a gold medal as Canada beat Sweden. It was a great start, but only the beginning for a player who would become as recognized as the winged wheel on his jersey.

4

Hard Times in Hockeytown

Detroit is a tough sports town. The fans love their teams. At times, they also love to hate their teams. Especially when they are losing. Many years had passed since the Wings brought home four Stanley Cups in the 1950s. Detroit fans were getting hungry again. The 1984-85 season held promise as Steve scored 30 goals and had 59 assists. This gave him two points beyond his production as a rookie. The team finished third in the Norris Division but was ousted by the Chicago Blackhawks in the first round of the playoffs. Still, Steve was seen as a valuable asset to the team and on his way to becoming a star player.

The 1985-86 season was a disappointment. A little more than halfway through, Steve had tallied only 14 goals and 28 assists. For a player of his ability, it fell short of the mark. Then, in a game against St. Louis,

Steve fractured his collarbone. It was his first major injury and he missed the rest of the season. Coaching duties split between Harry Neale and Brad Park gave the Wings only 17 wins in 80 games. The Wings finished in last place, not even making the playoffs.

In an attempt to get the Wings back on their feet, the club hired coach Jacques Demers. Demers brought new enthusiasm to the job and capitalized on the Wings' assets. One of those assets was Steve, one of the strongest players on the roster. In a bold move, Demers named Steve his team captain at training camp that fall. At 21, he was the youngest captain in Red Wings history and in the NHL.

"It kind of caught me off guard," says Steve. "Jacques Demers was just named coach of the team. When he first came, he called me into his office and said, 'I want to name you captain. What do you think?' I was surprised. I didn't expect it. Looking back, it was good for me because it really made me reassess. I had come off a difficult year, a bad year. I'd gotten off to a poor start. Then, when I finally started playing better, I got injured and missed the last 30 games of the year.

"But becoming the captain really made me work a little bit harder. I came to practice every day with the attitude that I was going to get something out of it. [I thought] 'I'm going to practice hard and, in the games, I'm going to compete hard.' It really made me focus on hockey."

Demers' style brought about other changes in Steve's role on the team. Scoring goals and dishing out assists would be only two pieces of the puzzle.

"He's the one who really started to use me more in a role," says Steve. "I still played the offensive part of the game, but he started to use me for killing penalties and **face-offs**. Our team was expected to keep the goals against (**goals-against average**) down, and soon, we were all expected to play in both ends of the rink."

That season the Wings improved, finishing second in the Norris Division standings. Their record went from a miserable 17-57-6 to a more respectable 34-36-10. They made it all the way to the Campbell Conference finals, where they lost to the Edmonton Oilers, eventual

Face-offs are a key role in which Steve excels for the Wings. He takes one here against the New Jersey Devils.

winners of the Stanley Cup. Steve was the key to the Wings' playoff success, leading the team with five goals and 13 assists.

Things continued to look up as Steve entered the 1987-88 season. He dominated the scoreboard, getting 49 goals in the first 63 games. Then, as Cynthia Lambert of *The Detroit News* wrote, "The worst thing that could possibly happen to the Red Wings happened..."

During the second period of a 4-0 win over the Buffalo Sabres, March 1, 1988, Steve slid into the goalpost. He injured his right knee and ended his best regular season to date. Earlier in the period, Steve scored his 50th goal of the season. He set a club record by scoring 50 goals in fewer games than any other Red Wing. Steve also had an assist, giving him 102 points, 40 more than any teammate at the time. After being taken to Detroit's Hutzel Hospital, Steve was told he had severely strained his **posterior cruciate ligament**. Many people thought his season was over.

But Steve never doubted himself. Choosing not to have surgery on the knee, he worked hard to rehabilitate the muscles surrounding it. He worked out in the team's weight room twice a day.

"I never once thought I wouldn't be able to play

again," Steve remembers. "At the time, I was concerned that it may shorten my career. That was about all. I wasn't too worried about that one."

Steve kept himself occupied by continuing his daily workouts and, during the playoffs, writing columns for

Steve puts the puck past Chicago Blackhawks goalie Ed Belfour.

the *Detroit Free Press*. Although Steve was disappointed that he wasn't playing, he did get to share his thoughts and insights with fans as the Wings fought their way through the post-season.

The Wings made it to the Campbell Conference finals, once again facing the Edmonton Oilers. Edmonton won the first two games of the series on its home ice. The crowd in Detroit's Joe Louis Arena showed its appreciation with thunderous applause when Steve, The Captain, unexpectedly returned to the lineup for a 5-2 win in Game 3. But the Oilers would prevail. They beat Detroit the next two games and went on to win their fourth Stanley Cup in five years.

For two more years, Demers tried to make Detroit a champion. The Wings had greatly improved the first two seasons he coached. But in 1989 they lost in the first round of the playoffs and in 1990 failed to qualify, finishing last in the Norris Division. The next season the Wings hired coach Bryan Murray, who did not meet management's expectations. Although Detroit had drafted many players who offered more support to Steve on the ice, he continued to be the team's best player. Offensively, he carried the weight of the Detroit Red Wings on his back. From 1987-88 through 1992-93, Steve had more than 100 points every season, including career highs of 155 points and 65 goals in 1988-89, but it wasn't enough. The Wings continued to lose in the playoffs, always ending their season long before the Stanley Cup was hoisted into the air by another NHL team.

Still, a series of difficult, frustrating seasons seemed to be coming to a close. The Wings continued to build with players such as Sergei Fedorov, Nicklas Lidstrom and Ray Sheppard. Through it all, Steve remained a constant. He quietly went about the business of scoring goals and keeping Detroit in contention for the Cup. With consistent play, great composure, a number of club records and a rehabilitated knee, Steve had shown just what kind of player he was: a true hockey professional full of perseverance and determination. It was something hockey fans would see again and again as Steve continued his own quest for the Cup.

5

The Bowman Era

Over the years, Scotty Bowman earned the reputation of being a tough coach. By 1993, he had also earned seven Stanley Cup rings, six of those as a head coach. In 1991, he was inducted into the Hockey Hall of Fame.

Detroit had fared well in recent seasons but seemed to stumble when playoff time came. The club decided it was time for another coaching change. This time, it wanted a coach whose record showed he could finish the job. The Wings believed that coach was Scotty Bowman.

While Steve enjoyed many accomplishments in his 10 seasons as a Red Wing, he had yet to guide his team to a Stanley Cup win. For him, it was the only true measure of success. Years of falling short started to take a toll on the young captain. Perhaps Bowman's experience and Steve's determination would combine for that winning result.

Before Bowman's arrival, in 1993, Detroit acquired players who would set the stage for some serious runs at the Stanley Cup. Sergei Fedorov and Dino Ciccarelli added some offensive punch while Nicklas Lidstrom and Vladimir Konstantinov anchored the defense. Now, with Bowman taking over the team, expectations were high that the Wings would surpass the improvements made by Jacques Demers and Bryan Murray. Bowman admits he had a strong club the first year he coached in Detroit.

"They had a high-scoring team," Bowman remembers. "They had a lot of good, young players that were in their developmental years. I more or less wanted to get a defensive system in place and get the goals against down. Their offense was strong."

Bowman also realized he had a quality player when he watched Steve.

"He was a great talent," Bowman says. "You know, a strength is talent plus work ethic. They're the two components you have to have and he had both of them."

But Bowman didn't get to see the depth of Steve's talent that first year. Steve's contributions were once again minimized by injury. In a game against the Winnipeg Jets October 21, 1993, Steve was hit from behind by Thomas Steen and crashed into the boards. A **herniated disk** would cause Steve to miss 26 games. Unlike his previous injuries, Steve was concerned about this one.

"When I had the surgery on my neck, that one made me a little bit nervous," says Steve. "I thought, 'I am going to come back from this, but am I going to be a good player again? Am I going to be able to take a solid hit?' It took me a little bit longer to really feel comfortable after that injury."

John Wharton, athletic trainer for the Wings, was concerned too. He remembers the surgery as if it were yesterday.

"He herniated a disk on his **cervical spine**," Wharton recalls. "They took a two-inch chunk of bone from his hip and placed it where the disk would be. Following that you've got to be in a **halo** and pretty much immobilize the neck for two months. After that, it's a very grueling, strenuous program of strengthening the spine, increasing the range of motion and getting your function back. Real simple things, [such] as looking to the left or looking to the right while you're driving, were a chore for him."

Wharton says that Steve exceeded the expectations for recovery.

"The immobilization period, I think, was the toughest for him," Wharton says. "He's so used to being an active person. But true to Stevie's form with every injury he's had, he really worked hard. I think he was ready about two months before he would have normally been, if he was an average person. Once he gets the green light to strengthen and rehab, he does it as quick and as efficiently as anybody I have ever seen."

But Wharton also knows there were reasons for Steve's quick healing.

"Looking after yourself and having a high threshold for pain are two things that make you an excellent candidate to be a quick healer," Wharton says. "He really looks after his body. He eats the right things. He gets the right amount of rest. He knows his body very well so he can get by with the amount of pain he can tolerate for certain situations."

Back on the ice, Sergei Fedorov would take Steve's place as center on the Wings' number one line. He also took over the duties of captain. The new depth of the Red Wings started to show as the team went about winning without Steve's help. When he returned to the lineup, Steve was still a key player. In his 58 games that season, Steve scored 24 goals and added 58 assists for 82 points.

The Wings led all NHL teams in scoring with 356 goals during Bowman's first year behind the bench. They finished in first place and felt confident about their chances going into the playoffs. Even the fans felt confident when they realized Detroit's first-round opponent was the San Jose Sharks. The Sharks had been in the league only three years and were seeded eighth in the playoffs.

The Wings were surprised by the Sharks' tenacity. The series seesawed for the entire seven games. A 4-0 shutout by Wings goalie Chris Osgood in Game 2 and a 7-1 rout by the Wings in Game 6 could not provide enough momentum to carry the team. The Wings lost the series at home on April 30 as the Sharks beat them 3-2.

Stunned by an early loss to a supposedly inferior team, the Wings tried to regroup. Throughout the off-season, Detroit fans and media chastised the Wings' players and staff. Bowman was viewed as nothing more than an expensive replacement for men who had done the same mediocre job years before. Steve and his teammates were seen as overpaid, over-indulged players who couldn't get the job done.

June editions of Detroit newspapers were heavy with rumors of trading The Captain. The rumors also included a number of his teammates. Steve decided to sit back and let the trade talk take its course. The pain in his back and neck from the October collision with Steen had continued through the season. Ignoring the rumors, he focused on getting healthy and being ready to play that fall. It was the best thing he could have done. To ease the pain in his back and neck, surgery was scheduled that summer. It helped stop the rumors. None of the other teams would want to buy a player with that kind of injury. There would be three to five months of rehabilitation and no guarantee what he would be capable of afterward.

While Steve went through his rehabilitation, Bowman set out to create a new game plan for the next season. Associate coach Barry Smith, returning from a coaching stint in Sweden, suggested a defensive system, the "left wing lock", that European teams were using. Bowman and associate coach Dave Lewis agreed.

"It's a basic system where you have three guys back," says Lewis. "It's usually the **forward** back on the left side of the rink. You're trying to prevent an attack and, if you can, create turnovers in the **neutral zone**."

At training camp that fall, Steve listened to merits of the new strategy. It would mean making some changes in his playing style. Although individual statistics might fall, the Wings would have fewer goals scored against them. This would generate more wins. As always, Steve looked at the bigger picture. His statistics didn't matter. What mattered was winning the Stanley Cup. Putting the team first, Steve dedicated himself to playing and promoting the left wing lock. Coach Smith recognized the effort Steve put into applying this system.

"I think Stevie knows that to stay in this league and be a top performer, you have to play both ends," Smith says. "The game has changed now and the recognition goes to those players who play well defensively, not just offensively. He was able to work on his game. He had the skills to do it before, he just wasn't asked to do it."

Camp went well. The Wings were eager to start the season armed with their new weapon. However, NHL team owners had another idea. Fueled by the rise in players' salaries, many teams were experiencing financial problems. The players and owners could not agree on a contract. When the exhibition season ended, the owners created a lock of their own. For 103 days, teams were locked out and not allowed to play. After the sides came to an agreement, the NHL season started January 20, 1995. It was decided each team would play only 48 games, all against teams in the same conference.

Steve revisited Bowman's comments from training camp. He reviewed Dick Todd's philosophy at Peter-

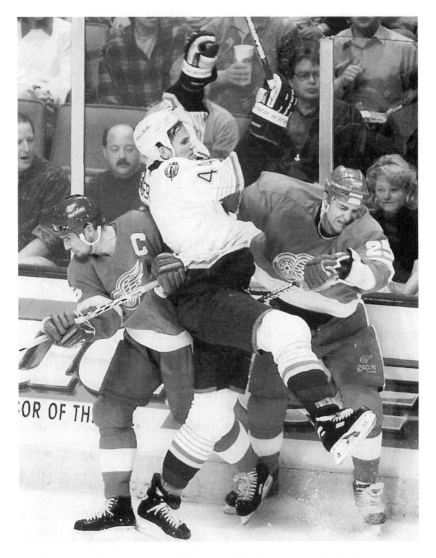

**Steve and teammate Darren McCarty sandwich
St. Louis Blues' defenseman Chris Pronger.**

borough. His game would become more defense ori-

ented. Individual statistics would be sacrificed for the

good of the team. Even better, the rest of the Red Wings stood by The Captain with the same belief. As difficult as it might be, Steve was ready to make that sacrifice.

"When Scotty came in, he totally changed it," Steve remembers. "It became, 'I don't care how many goals we get, if we get five goals or 50 goals, I better be able to count on you guys every game, defensively, every shift. You've got to be good defensively.' So the difficult part was to see your statistics come down. Everybody's saying, 'He's not the player he once was... time to trade him; get something while we still can. He doesn't score like he used to.' They want you to be a good defensive player, but you're not producing. You're doing what you're expected to do, what they (the coaches) want you to do."

At the end of the shortened season, the results of Bowman's strategies were obvious. The Wings won the Presidents' Trophy, awarded to the team with the NHL's best regular-season record (33 wins, 11 losses, 4 ties). They skated easily through the playoffs, ending the Dallas Stars' season in five games, the San Jose Sharks' in four, and the Chicago Blackhawks' in five. For the first time since 1966, the Detroit Red Wings were going to the Stanley Cup finals.

Steve finally saw his dreams becoming reality. The team had dominated through the regular season and the playoffs. The Wings were favored to win it all. Despite suffering a knee injury in the second round of the play-offs, Steve was playing and ready to take on the New Jersey Devils.

But it was not meant to be. The Wings were swept by the Devils in four games. Steve played well but not at the top of his game due to the injury. He scored only one goal in a series in which his team was outscored 16-7. With the rest of the Wings, Steve once again returned to Detroit greatly disappointed. His only hope, as before: next season.

6

The Fans Speak

The summer of 1995 was a long one. It was long for Scotty Bowman. He knew more changes had to be made. It was long for Steve Yzerman. He returned to the Wings' camp that season with an uncertain future.

Trade rumors surrounded Steve once again. His back and knee injuries were completely rehabilitated. He was a healthy center with solid statistics. There was no up-coming surgery, as there had been in 1994. Detroit could easily put Steve up for trade. The Senators, from his hometown of Ottawa, were seriously looking to acquire him. True to his style, Steve did not seek attention from teammates, management or the media by pleading his case to stay in Detroit. He quietly went about his job and resigned himself to the fact that this was business.

"Everybody handles things a different way," Steve says. "I know how this business works and you're going to go to a team that isn't going to win it in the next few years. The biggest reason I didn't want to be traded was I was going from one of the best teams in the league to wherever I was going to be traded. It wasn't going to be a good team. So my approach was 'I'm going to play. I'm going to play well. And whatever happens happens.'"

As the date of the Wings' home opener neared, Steve's status had not changed. Steve donned his Wings **sweater** October 13, 1995. At the pre-game ceremonies, the team was awarded banners for its previous season's accomplishments: the Presidents' Trophy, the Western Conference title and the Central Division title. As the banners rippled in the rafters of Joe Louis Arena, announcer Budd Lynch introduced the team. When he read, "Number 19… Steve Yzerman," the fans responded with a deafening ovation. They stood and chanted, "Stevie! Stevie! Stevie!" for well over a minute. Detroit fans had spoken. They wanted the Stanley Cup. They did not want to win it without their captain. Although Steve felt it was a nice gesture, he also knew fan support alone wouldn't keep him in Detroit.

"It was really nice," Steve says. "I appreciated it. But the reason I stayed is because I played well. If I hadn't played well, I would have been traded. I had to produce. I feel I did that."

Still, Scotty Bowman seemed to get the fans' message. The trade rumors ended and Detroit began a season of domination in the NHL. The Wings pummeled team after team, racking up a record-setting 62 wins in the regular season. They scored 325 goals to their opponents' 181. Steve scored 95 points (36 goals, 59 assists). Once again, the Wings were the team to beat. They were heavily favored to win the Cup as the playoffs started.

Round 1 was against the Winnipeg Jets. The Wings outscored the Jets 20-10 in the series. With all that offense, it still took Detroit six games to end the Jets' season.

St. Louis stretched the Wings even further in Round 2. The Wings opened the series with a confident 2-0 lead. They stifled Brett Hull and shut down Wayne Gretzky, leaving the Blues looking old and weary. Game 3 changed everything. An overtime win gave new life to the Blues. They went on to win the next two games, putting the series at 3-2. Facing elimination, the Wings mustered every ounce of energy they had left. They won a tough 4-2 decision, forcing a Game 7 back in Detroit. In the first six games, Steve scored four goals (three of those a **natural hat trick** in Game 3) and assisted on three others. But none of these points would compare to the one he was yet to get. It produced one of the most memorable moments of Steve's career.

The score remained 0-0 through three periods of regulation play and one period of overtime. Fans in Joe Louis Arena held their breath with every shot on goal. About a minute into the second overtime, Steve snatched the puck from Gretzky and, near the **blue line**, sent a **slap shot** whizzing past Blues goalie Jon Casey. The goal stunned Casey and the Blues. It also surprised The Captain.

"I shot it and looked up and heard the clang against the bar," Steve told *Detroit Free Press* reporter Viv Bernstein, "and I was like, 'No way. It went in!'"

The Wings' players mobbed their captain, celebrat-

Buried under a pile of happy teammates, the Wings celebrate Steve's game winning goal in double-overtime against St. Louis during the 1996 playoffs.

ing the 1-0 victory. They were heading to the Western Conference finals.

Steve and his teammates didn't have long to revel in the victory. Three days later, the Colorado Avalanche stormed into Joe Louis Arena. With incredible size and speed, the Avalanche quickly took a 2-0 lead in the series on Detroit's home ice. Detroit headed to Denver determined to show the Avalanche it would not roll over and die. The Wings came out shooting in Game 3, earning a 6-4 win. But Game 4 would put Detroit in an all too familiar situation. After a 4-2 loss, Detroit headed home facing elimination. The Wings fought back with a 5-2 victory. Did they have back-to-back wins in them? The team thought so. Detroit fans hoped so. Tension kept building as the series moved back to Colorado. Yet nothing could prepare the Wings or their fans for what was to come.

From the opening face-off, Game 6 had all the beginnings of a new NHL rivalry. The players battled. The

During the 1996 Game 6 loss to the Avs, a Colorado fan reminds Steve how long it has been since a Red Wing hoisted the Stanley Cup.

coaches, who had traded criticism in the news media, argued across the benches. This game would come to characterize all future meetings between the two teams. The event that pushed the rivalry front and center was Claude Lemieux's hit from behind on Wings center Kris Draper. Slammed into the boards face first, Draper suffered a series of facial fractures and a broken jaw. Even with the motivation of revenge for Draper, the Wings lost the game 4-1. Colorado went on to beat the Florida Panthers in a four-game sweep and hoist the Stanley Cup.

Once again, Steve's season ended short of his goal. He led his team in the playoffs, scoring eight goals and adding 12 assists. He scored his 500th goal, January 17, 1996, against Colorado during the regular season.

But that didn't matter.

Personal statistics never mattered.

What mattered was whether or not your team won the Stanley Cup.

Next season, Steve and his teammates would try again.

7

Lord Stanley's Cup

It had been 42 years since the Stanley Cup had called the city of Detroit home. After seeing the Cup within reach the two previous seasons, Steve and the Wings pushed even harder. The 1996-97 season would be different. It had to be.

During the off-season, Steve played for Team Canada in the World Cup of Hockey tournament. During the tournament, he was impressed by the play of fellow Canadian Brendan Shanahan. Shanahan was a power forward with a wicked shot. A couple of months later, Steve got the opportunity to play again with Shanahan. This time it was with the Wings. The day of their home opener, October 9, the Wings sent Keith Primeau and Paul Coffey, along with a number one draft pick, to the Hartford Whalers. In exchange, Shanahan arrived at Joe Louis Arena just as the Wings were about to head onto the ice for warm-ups.

"It was a whirlwind day," remembers Shanahan. "The Wings basically called me up and said, 'Go to the airport and we'll have our plane waiting there. The deal's not done yet but we hope it will be done by the time you land in Detroit. If not, we'll fly you home.'"

The Wings waited a few extra minutes for Shanahan to dress. Then, as a team, they all came onto the ice. Although he didn't score, he was a versatile left **wing** on the ice for power plays and penalty killing. His contributions helped Detroit beat the Oilers 2-0, stopping their three-game winning streak.

As the season rolled on, the Wings seemed to take everything in stride. Scotty Bowman seemed to switch his lines every game. No one argued. Each of the Wings went out on the ice every night and played the role he was asked to play, following Steve's example.

"One of the best things about playing hockey with Steve," Shanahan says, "is the fact that he shows up every night to play. You never have to worry about your linemate taking a night off. Every night he shows up to play his best."

Early in November, Steve signed a four-year contract. It compensated him as one of the Wings' top players, and assured him a place in Wings management when his playing career ended. In February, Steve passed another milestone when he played his 1,000th NHL game. As the season came to a close, Steve turned in another respectable set of statistics with 22 goals and 63 assists for 85 points.

Although the Wings seemed confident, they did not dominate as they had previously in the regular season. Their record was third best in the Western Conference at 38-26-18. Perhaps the Wings had finally put the regular season in perspective. It was important to play well and get a decent **playoff berth**. It was more important for the team to turn up the intensity and narrow its focus during the playoffs. Everything was falling into place.

Their first victim would be the St. Louis Blues. The teams split the first two games in Detroit. In St. Louis, Steve scored on the power play in Game 3 as the Wings won 3-2. Blues goalie Grant Fuhr got his second shutout of the series in Game 4, but the Wings' 5-2 win in Game 5 put St. Louis one game from elimination. The Wings ended the series two nights later with a 3-1 win at Joe Louis Arena.

The second round brought the Anaheim Mighty Ducks. Games 1 and 2 combined for four periods of overtime but Detroit got the deciding goal in each. Down 2-0 in Game 3, the Wings rallied back to win 5-3. They finally swept the series in Game 4 with a 3-2 win in double overtime.

Round 3 brought back the rivalry everyone wanted to see. The Wings vs. Colorado, the defending Stanley Cup champion. While fans and the media played up the angle of revenge for Kris Draper, Steve remembers it was not the team's focus.

"We weren't talking about that," Steve says. "We weren't focused on Claude Lemieux. They had too many other players. We just wanted to beat Colorado. We wanted to win."

The Avalanche took advantage of home ice, winning 2-1 in the first game. Leading the comeback in

Game 2, Steve scored the game winner as the Wings won 4-2. The Wings won the next two games, shocking the Avs 6-0 in Game 4. But Colorado wasn't finished. Back home, the Avs got back into the series, repeating the 6-0 score.

Now it was Detroit's turn to make home ice an advantage. The Wings eliminated Colorado with a 3-1 victory. Steve accepted the Campbell Conference bowl, quickly acknowledged the crowd, and skated off the ice. It was another game won. The Wings had at least four more to go. It was time to take on the Philadelphia Flyers in the Stanley Cup finals.

The Flyers were a big, hard-hitting team. Detroit was ready for them. The Wings played smart and skated fast throughout Game 1. Detroit led 3-2 after two periods. Then, just 56 seconds into the third period, Steve wound up for a slap shot from the blue line, beating Flyers goalie Ron Hextall. Breaking with tradition, the Wings took Game 1 of the series, 4-2, in Philadelphia. The Wings had not won a game in the finals since April 26, 1966, when they beat the Montreal Canadiens for a

2-0 lead in the series. But those Wings had lost the Cup four games later. This was just the first of many traditions to be broken.

The Wings returned for a repeat performance in Philadelphia three nights later. The Flyers started goalie Garth Snow after Hextall's weak performance in Game 1. It didn't seem to matter. Steve put the Wings ahead early in the first period with a power-play goal. Shanahan scored two goals and Kirk Maltby added another as Detroit won 4-2. It was an enviable position. The Wings were heading back to Detroit with a 2-0 lead, knowing they could very well win the Stanley Cup at home.

Steve got the Wings' first goal of Game 3 on a power play. As the Wings racked up goals, the Detroit fans cheered every hit, pass or blocked shot by a player in red and white. When it was over, the scoreboard flashed a 6-1 Wings victory. Steve was one game away from his lifetime dream. But Bowman told reporters his team would have little time to enjoy the victory.

"We're three-fourths of the way there, that's the way I look at it," Bowman said. "I told the players to enjoy the win for five minutes, then start thinking about the next game."

And think they did. Nicklas Lidstrom slapped a shot

Steve and Wings celebrate Detroit's first Stanley Cup in 42 years. The Wings swept the Philadelphia Flyers in four games.

home in the first period of Game 4 for a 1-0 lead. In the second period, Darren McCarty faked out a **defenseman** and then Hextall, putting Detroit up 2-0. The score held well into the third period until Hextall, the Flyers' goalie, headed toward the bench to give Philadelphia another attacker. With 14.8 seconds left in the game, Eric Lindros scored his only goal of the series for the Flyers. It was too little, too late. Fifteen seconds later, the Wings were celebrating a 2-1 victory and a sweep of the Flyers.

NHL commissioner Gary Bettman met Steve at center ice. As the crowd cheered, he presented Steve with the Stanley Cup. Steve hoisted the Cup high and turned to his team to share the honor. But his teammates had a different idea.

"He had

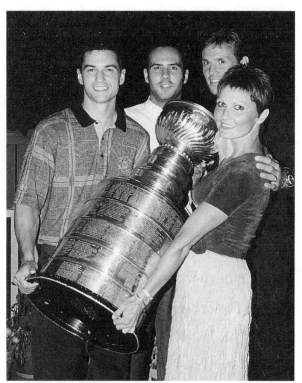

Following Detroit's first Stanley Cup championship in 42 years, Steve (second from right) celebrates back home in Nepean with his sister Roni-Jean and brothers Gary and Christopher.

suffered so many defeats and had shouldered a lot of the responsibility in previous years," Shanahan recalls. "He turned to bring the Cup over to the team and we all pointed for him to take a lap himself because he had earned it. It was a great moment to be his teammate."

Steve started his skate around the rink. He looked for his parents and his wife in the stands. Part way around the ice, he stopped in front of Mike Ilitch, letting him raise the trophy high. After 14 long and often difficult years, Steve's dream had become a reality.

"I don't know how to describe how I feel," Steve told reporters. "I'm glad the game is over, but I wish it never ended."

Looking back, associate coach Dave Lewis, like all the members of the Wings organization, remembers how special it was seeing Steve with the Cup.

"A favorite Yzerman moment?" he asks. "It's when he held the Stanley Cup over his head. Prior to that season, Steve was criticized locally and nationally for not being a leader, not being able to lead his team to victory. He was taking a lot of unfair criticism. I was so happy to see him raise that Cup over his head."

Steve looked forward to a summer in which he would be in the very position he had seen Wayne Gretzky and Mario Lemieux enjoy. No one could take away the pride and feeling of accomplishment brought about by winning a Stanley Cup.

But the celebrations of Steve and his teammates *would* be cut short . . .

8

Back "TWO" Back

Less than a week after the Wings won the Stanley Cup, a tragedy befell them. Teammates Vladimir Konstantinov and Slava Fetisov and team **masseur** Sergei Mnatsakanov were returning home after a golf outing in Washington Township, Michigan, Friday, June 13, 1997. The driver of their limousine crashed into a tree, injuring all three men. By Sunday, Fetisov was listed in good condition while Konstantinov and Mnatsakanov remained critical. After only six days of celebrations and parades, Steve returned to his role as captain and spoke for all the Wings players at a hospital news conference.

"Our entire organization is devastated by the accident," Steve said to reporters. "We request that you respect the privacy of the families and members of the organization. The players feel it is not appropriate to give out interviews because we don't quite understand everything that's involved and we prefer to let the doctors answer all those questions. We ask everyone's support and prayers for our teammate, Vladdie, and trainer, Sergei."

That September, the Wings returned to training camp for the 1997-98 season. Many of the Wings told the media that the season would be dedicated to keeping the Stanley Cup in honor of their injured teammates. Throughout the season, the team's sweaters bore patches that honored Konstantinov and Mnatsakanov. It reminded all the Wings that, although it was great to win, other things in life mattered more.

"Every time I thought about it, it was very saddening," Steve said of the accident. "It really kept things in perspective after we won. It brought everybody back down to earth, not just the hockey players but the Red Wing fans as well. It was absolutely the most important thing to win the Cup. Then you realize, after this terrible accident, there are more important things than winning. If you can take anything out of that accident that helped us, it's that any time there was heat or pressure on us, we were comfortable. We had the accident to remind us, 'Don't make more out of this than it is. Go out and play and it's not life or death.'"

That philosophy remained in Steve's mind the entire season. As the Wings played through another admirable season, Steve continued to break records, pass milestones and take advantage of opportunities.

Less than a month into the season, Steve moved up the list of NHL all-time scorers. In a 4-3 win over the San Jose Sharks, Steve scored goal number 544. He was tied for 15th place with Montreal Canadiens great Maurice "Rocket" Richard.

A few weeks later, Steve found out he would play for Team Canada in the 1998 Winter Olympics. He went to Nagano, Japan, as the **assistant captain** for the team, excited about the opportunity to represent his country. It was an experience he hasn't forgotten.

"I loved the atmosphere there," says Steve. "You were mingling with athletes from all over the world, getting to see guys who had just won a gold medal. The games were tough and we had a difficult loss to the Czechs, but it was a great experience."

Many of the Canadian hockey players brought their

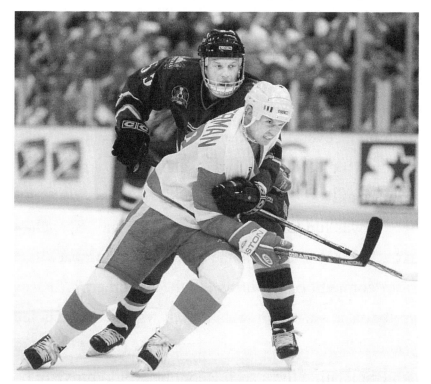

Steve fights off the Washington Capitals' Sergei Gonchar during the 1998 Stanley Cup Finals.

families to Japan. They took in tourist attractions and spent time shopping. However, Steve's wife, Lisa, was home awaiting the birth of their second child. Although Steve took his Olympic ice time seriously, he also tried to find ways to have fun away from the rink. He and teammate Brendan Shanahan found one way. They were known for raiding the Olympic Village cafeteria for ice cream late at night.

"There wasn't a whole lot to do around there at night," Steve chuckles. "The food at the cafeteria was from all over the world; they had to please everybody, a little bit of everything. So we'd hang out and go there around 10 o'clock. Ice cream seemed like a good bedtime snack!"

"It was fun to go down to the cafeteria," Shanahan says. "You would see some athletes coming back late from competition." But as for the ice cream? "It was pretty basic – a scoop of vanilla. It was the only choice you had."

But beating the Czech Republic would prove to be much more difficult than finding flavors of ice cream. Team Canada would bow out in the semifinals, losing to the Czechs 2-1. Steve had a goal and an assist in six Olympic games. These games were the spark that fueled a flame. When Steve returned to Detroit, he began to focus on finishing the NHL season with another Stanley Cup. The mid-winter break seemed to be just what he needed. By the end of March, Steve led the Wings with 61 points. In a game against the Chicago Blackhawks, with the Wings down by three goals, Steve scored two goals and added two assists. The 5-5 tie clinched a playoff spot for the Wings. In the next game, Steve got his 1,400th career point and 561st goal, passing Guy Lafleur for 12th place in goals. The Wings finished the season 44-23-15, second to Dallas in the Central Division and Western Conference.

In playoffs, the Wings beat Phoenix, St. Louis and finally Dallas to secure another spot in the Stanley Cup finals. Once again, the Wings showed their depth and determination, sweeping the Washington Capitals in four games. Steve raised the Stanley Cup and the Conn Smythe Trophy, which recognized him as the playoffs' Most Valuable Player. Even with the individual recognition, Steve felt it was winning that second Stanley Cup that validated his long career.

"The most important accomplishment is playing on

Voted Most Valuable Player of the 1998 playoffs, Steve is awarded the Conn Smythe Trophy.

two Stanley Cup winners," Steve says. "That, to me, makes everything else insignificant. The fact that I was able to play on a team that's won two Cups and it's been the same organization that I have been with my whole career makes it more meaningful. I've put in a lot of time and effort to be a part of it, to be part of the team growing to be a *successful* team."

And so the parades and celebrations honoring Steve and his champion teammates started again. This time, they would last all summer.

9

The Road Ahead

It has been two seasons since the Wings won the Stanley Cup. Steve and the Wings made the playoffs both seasons, but they lost in the second round. Steve continues to be the Wings' top center. He also continues to lead as their captain in his quiet and unassuming way. His years in the NHL give him strengths that go beyond the basics of goal scoring or defense.

"I understand the game," Steve says. "I can adapt. I see a situation and do what I need to do."

But ask opponents what makes Steve a threat and they will tell you much more. Colorado Avalanche assistant coach Bryan Trottier has seen firsthand the damage Steve can do. Although Steve idolized him as a youngster, it's clear Trottier feels Steve has excelled well beyond Trottier's accomplishments as an NHL superstar.

"Steve surpasses me in puck control and stick handling," Trottier says. "He has a much better shot than I ever had, in accuracy and power. He has prided himself in his defensive game, for example face-offs, positioning and blocking shots, as well as back-checking."

As a coach, Trottier sees Steve as a tough opponent for a number of reasons.

"He is almost impossible to contain," Trottier says. "He can hurt you with his scoring or passing and he'll burn a defenseman with his stick handling. He wins so many face-offs, his team has the puck most of the night. His competitive drive and proud play will not allow him to give up. He works for 60 minutes, which makes him one of the great leaders of all time. As a fan and a coach, I see a gifted competitive athlete with skills of the highest level in every fundamental aspect of the game."

Darren Pang, his friend and former teammate in Nepean, agrees that Steve's hard work has helped put him in the NHL's elite.

"Watch how often after practice he stays out there and is one of the last guys to leave the ice," Pang says.

"He's working on face-offs, working on shooting, and working on **deking**. That's one thing that really stands out to me. It's the pride he takes in his work ethic. Then, when he gets on the ice, I would say he's currently one of the very best face-off men that there is in the game. He is, in my opinion, the best shot-blocking forward in the NHL. And besides, he's got the uncanny ability to just score big goals."

Jimmy Devellano agrees that Steve is one of a kind.

"I think he was the most important pick we made," Devellano says, looking back. "It was my first draft and we had an awful hockey team. The players we would draft in 1983 were hopefully going to be the building blocks for the future of the team. As it turns out, taking Yzerman fourth overall… he certainly became more than a building block. He became the pillar that the franchise was built around. Sometimes it pays to be lucky."

Although Steve is probably best known for his hard work on the ice, he is just as dedicated in his off-ice pursuits. Throughout his years in Detroit, Steve has been involved with a number of local charities. He has donated his time at hockey camps and, though not well publicized, he has been a frequent visitor to children in area hospitals.

"I've gotten to know a few of them quite well," he says. "Some have had battles with cancer, and beat it, fortunately. A couple of the kids I got involved with unfortunately passed away because of their illness."

But Steve views the situation positively.

"It's been especially rewarding for me because you have some influence on the kid and brighten their day a little bit," he says. "I have gotten to see how some of these kids deal with their problems. It's remarkable how tough they are. They deal with the adversity much better than some of the adults, myself included. We have problems far less than what they face."

Steve's family is also important to him. He lives in suburban Detroit with his wife, Lisa, and their three daughters, Isabella, Maria and Sophia. Steve feels making time for his family is not only a priority, it actually helps his hockey playing.

"I enjoy being home," Steve says. "There are two

Steve is recognized during a pre-game ceremony at Joe Louis Arena for scoring his 500th goal during the 1995-96 season. His wife Lisa and daughter Isabella join him.

things right now: my family and hockey. I just go to the rink and practice or play and then I come home. When you're struggling or your team's not playing well, you really have a tendency to over-think and get so wrapped up in it that it just doesn't help you at all. Having a family gives me the chance to forget about it and come to the rink really fresh the next day."

Although his family and hockey take up most of his time, Steve squeezes in a few other favorite activities. He's an avid golfer and likes to do crossword puzzles. He also enjoys boating and hitting the waves on a Sea-Doo when spending time at his summer cottage north of Toronto. He and Lisa also enjoy going to movies.

At age 35, Steve continues to put the finishing touches on his Hall of Fame career in Detroit. During the 1999-2000 season, Steve scored 35 goals and had 44 assists for 79 points. One of those goals, scored November 26, 1999, against Edmonton, was his 600th. An assist in a game November 17, 1999, against Vancouver was his 900th. He was awarded the Frank J. Selke Trophy as the NHL's best defensive forward. He carries on a captaincy that has reigned well over 1,000 games and 14 seasons. But Steve also realizes he can't play hockey, or be the captain, forever.

"I think in the near future it will be time for another

guy to come in and be the captain of the team," Steve says. "As some of the younger guys on our team mature, they're kind of taking over and they become the voice of, or the pulse of, the team. My group is becoming older now. I'm more of a veteran and my role is going to slowly decrease."

But many people believe Steve is playing some of the best hockey of his career. They wonder what else Steve will add to his stellar list of achievements. He has set team and league records, won individual awards, has made nine All-Star appearances, represented his country in international competition, and had his name inscribed on the Stanley Cup twice. He continues to amaze hockey fans and inspire his teammates and coaches.

"He's definitely the epitome of the guy who goes out and leads by example," says teammate Darren McCarty. "He's one of the hardest working guys, not only on the ice but off the ice too. He does all the little things that need to be done."

Steve also sets a great example for younger players on the team.

"He has shown me that, through all his greatness and all the records, it's still the same guy that you would know if he didn't have all the records," says Mathieu Dandenault, a Wing for six seasons. "It doesn't get to his head. He takes it all in stride. It's amazing to watch, the point in his career where he's done everything, and he just keeps working at it, working hard to be better."

John Wharton, the Wings' trainer, agrees that Steve sets a good example. He never stops working to be the best.

"He's an elite athlete when it comes to conditioning and training," Wharton says. "It's great to have your captain in such good shape and with such a good work ethic because it filters down throughout the rest of the team. The younger guys come in and see the effort that Steve's putting out. He leads by example, on the ice and in the weight room."

Associate coach Dave Lewis offers similar praise.

"Every team would love to have a player like Steve Yzerman on their team and every coach would love to coach him," says Lewis. "That's a tribute to him and one of the greatest compliments you can give a player."

In January 1999, the Nepean Raiders honored Steve by renaming their home rink *The Steve Yzerman Arena*. The last contract he signed in Detroit made him a Red Wing for life, including a front office position once his playing career is over.

"I think I would like to be a general manager," Steve says. "I want to scout and help build a team. I like to follow players and the trades made and see if I can figure out why they did certain things. I enjoy picking out traits, seeing the building blocks that a player has."

Surely the Wings organization hopes that if he takes on that role, he can find them a player who will somehow compensate for the huge hole left in their roster. Number 19's skates will be difficult to fill.

Steve takes his good friend "Stanley" for a ride on his Sea-Doo.

Regular Season Statistics

Season	Team	League	Games Played	Goals	Assists	Points	Penalty Minutes
1981-82	Peterborough	OHL	58	21	43	64	65
1982-83	Peterborough	OHL	56	42	49	91	33
	Canada	**WJC-A**	7	2	3	5	2
1983-84	Detroit	NHL	80	39	48	87	33
1984-85	Canada	C Cup	4	0	0	0	0
	Detroit	NHL	80	30	59	89	58
	Canada	**WEC-A**	10	3	4	7	6
1985-86	Detroit	NHL	51	14	28	42	16
1986-87	Detroit	NHL	80	31	59	90	43
1987-88	Detroit	NHL	64	50	52	102	44
1988-89	Detroit	NHL	80	65	90	155	61
	Canada	WEC-A	8	5	7	12	2
1989-90	Detroit	NHL	79	62	65	127	79
	Canada	WEC-A	10	10	10	20	8
1990-91	Detroit	NHL	80	51	57	108	34
1991-92	Detroit	NHL	79	45	58	103	64
1992-93	Detroit	NHL	84	58	79	137	44
1993-94	Detroit	NHL	58	24	58	82	36
1995	Detroit	NHL	47	12	26	38	40
1995-96	Detroit	NHL	80	36	59	95	64
1996-97	Canada	W Cup	6	2	1	3	0
	Detroit	NHL	81	22	63	85	78
1997-98	Detroit	NHL	75	24	45	69	46
	Canada	Olympic	6	1	1	2	10
1998-99	Detroit	NHL	80	29	45	74	42
1999-00	Detroit	NHL	78	35	44	79	34

Playoff Statistics

Season	Team	League	Games Played	Goals	Assists	Points	Penalty Minutes
1981-82	Peterborough	OHL	6	0	1	1	16
1982-83	Peterborough	OHL	4	1	4	5	0
	Canada	WJC-A	-	-	-	-	-
1983-84	Detroit	NHL	4	3	3	6	0
1984-85	Canada	C Cup	-	-	-	-	-
	Detroit	NHL	3	2	1	3	2
	Canada	WEC-A	-	-	-	-	-
1985-86	Detroit	NHL	-	-	-	-	-
1986-87	Detroit	NHL	16	5	13	18	8
1987-88	Detroit	NHL	3	1	3	4	6
1988-89	Detroit	NHL	6	5	5	10	2
	Canada	WEC-A	-	-	-	-	-
1989-90	Detroit	NHL	-	-	-	-	-
	Canada	WEC-A	-	-	-	-	-
1990-91	Detroit	NHL	7	3	3	6	4
1991-92	Detroit	NHL	11	3	5	8	12
1992-93	Detroit	NHL	7	4	3	7	4
1993-94	Detroit	NHL	3	1	3	4	0
1995	Detroit	NHL	15	4	8	12	0
1995-96	Detroit	NHL	18	8	12	20	4
1996-97	Canada	W Cup	-	-	-	-	-
	Detroit	NHL	20	7	6	13	4
1997-98	Detroit	NHL	22	6	18	24	22
	Canada	Olympic	-	-	-	-	-
1998-99	Detroit	NHL	10	9	4	13	0
1999-00	Detroit	NHL	8	0	4	4	0

xiv

NHL Career Awards and Accomplishments
through 1999-2000 Season

- Scored a goal and an assist in NHL debut vs. Winnipeg (10-5-83)
- Reached 50-goal mark in fewer games (55) than any other Red Wing (1988-89)
- NHL All-Rookie Team (1984)
- Voted top rookie by *The Sporting News* (1984)
- Runner-up for 1983-84 Calder Trophy (NHL Rookie of the Year)
- First wore captain's "C" in 1986-87 at the age of 21, youngest in Wings history
- Longest serving captain in NHL history in terms of games and seasons
- Two club-record nine-game goal streaks, 12 goals, 11/18/88 through 12/5/88, and 14 goals, 1/29/92 through 2/12/92
- Club-record 28-game scoring streak, 29 goals, 36 assists, 11/1/88 through 1/4/89
- 1988-89 Lester B. Pearson Award as top performer by vote of NHL Players Association
- Recorded 1,000th point with an assist at Buffalo 2/24/93
- 18 regular-season hat tricks (most recent at Chicago 2/14/93); tied with Gordie Howe for club record

- Three natural hat tricks (most recent at Toronto 11/17/90)
- 1,300th point with goal at Chicago 1/5/97
- Had three assists in 1,000th career game, vs. Calgary 2/19/97
- 800th career assist was a game-winning assist vs. Buffalo 3/28/97
- Scored 1,400th career point on a power-play goal vs. Buffalo 3/29/98
- Represented Team Canada as assistant captain in 1998 Nagano Winter Olympics
- In 1998 Stanley Cup playoffs, led all NHL players with 24 points (6-18-24) in 22 games
- Awarded the Conn Smythe Trophy as playoff MVP (1998)
- Two Stanley Cup championships (1996-97, 1997-98)
- Recorded 900th career NHL assist 11/17/99 at Vancouver
- Recorded 1,500th career NHL point 11/20/99 at Edmonton
- Played in 1,200th career NHL game 11/24/99 at St. Louis

- Became 11th player in NHL history to score 600 goals 11/26/99 vs. Edmonton
- In NHL records, ranked 6th (tied with Mark Messier) in all-time goals (627), eighth in all-time assists (935) and 6th in all-time points (1,562) entering 2000-2001 season
- Yzerman had 627 goals in 1,256 games while Messier had 627 goals in 1,479 games
- 935 assists as a Red Wing is second only to Gordie Howe (1,023)
- Has led team in points 11 times, goals six times and assists 10 times
- Topped 100-point mark six times (one of 13 in NHL history to do it six times in a row)
- Scored 50 goals or more five times
- Scored 60 goals or more twice
- Club-record 49 shorthanded goals
- 10 All-Star Game selections (1984, '88-93, '97, '99, 2000) Did not play in 1999 All-Star Game due to injury
- Won the Frank J. Selke Trophy for Best Defensive Forward (1999-2000)

Glossary

assistant captain (also known as **alternate captain**) A player who may question the referees for his team while on the ice. A team appoints a captain and up to two assistant captains so one of these players can be on the ice at all times.

back-checking to hinder an opponent who is trying to reach his attacking zone.

blue line the two blue lines divide a hockey rink into three sections: a team's defending zone, the neutral zone, and the team's attacking zone.

bobskates skates with double blades on the bottom. Used by beginning skaters to improve their stability and balance.

center the center player in the forward, or attacking, line.

CJHL Central Junior Hockey League.

cervical spine The spine is made up of 33 bones. The top seven bones in the neck make up the cervical spine.

defenseman one of two players who play in or near the defensive zone to assist the goalkeeper.

deke/deking a faking motion made by a player carrying the puck.

face-off To start play at any time, the puck is dropped between two opposing players facing each other.

forward a member of the attacking line. The center, left wing and right wing are all forwards.

goals-against average the average number of goals scored against a goalkeeper in a game.

halo a rigid, molded plastic frame used to immobilize the head and neck after injury. It sits on the shoulders supporting the chin and back of the head, extending up around the skull. It keeps the person from moving the neck in any direction while the injury is healing.

hat trick when one player scores three goals in a game.

herniated disk Between each bone of the spine is a disk. Disks are like small water balloons that absorb shock. When a disk is herniated, or injured, the inside bulges out, pressing on the spinal nerves, causing pain.

house leagues teams made up of players who have not reached the level of play to earn spots on travel hockey teams. These players play in local games at their home arenas.

masseur a man whose work is massaging athletes as part of their training and fitness program.

natural hat trick when three goals are scored consecutively by the same player in the same game.

neutral zone the center ice area between the two blue lines. It is called the neutral zone because it is neither an attacking zone nor a defensive zone.

NHL National Hockey League. The league started in 1917 and currently has 30 teams.

NHL Entry Draft originally known as the NHL Amateur Draft. Players register with the NHL and if eligible, are placed on the availability list by the NHL Central Registry. Eligible players can then be selected to play for a team.

playoff berth Of the 30 teams in the NHL,

eight in each conference are awarded the chance to participate in the first round of the playoffs based on their regular season records.

posterior cruciate ligament One of the main ligaments of the knee, it holds two bones together, the tibia (shin bone) and the femur (thigh bone).

protected list a list of players who will be kept by a team. These players cannot be drafted to play for another team.

rookie an athlete playing his/her first year in a professional sport.

slap shot when a player takes his stick back and then quickly swings it forward, firing the puck toward the goal.

Stanley Cup   presented in 1893 by the Governor-General of Canada, Lord Stanley, as a trophy for the amateur hockey champions of Canada. Since 1910, it has recognized the champions of North America. Since 1926, only NHL teams have competed for it.

sweater   team shirt or jersey. In the early days of hockey, team shirts were sweaters made out of wool.

WEC-A   World & European Championship, Pool A. The top group of countries in the world (known as Pool A) compete for the World

Championship. The countries that make up the other pools (Pool B, Pool C and Pool D) play to qualify for promotion to the World Championship.

WJC-A   World Junior Championship, Pool A. This championship is similar to the World Championship, Pool A. The players compete in two age categories, under 20 or under 18.

wing or **winger**   a player who plays on either side of the center in the forward, or attacking, line.

Time Line

1965 Steve Yzerman is born on May 9 in Cranbrook, British Columbia.

1970 Attends his first hockey camp and joins his first organized team.

1975-81 Yzerman family moves to the Ottawa suburb of Nepean, Ontario. Steve plays two years of Junior A Tier 2 hockey in the Central Junior Hockey League for the Nepean Raiders.

1981-83 Drafted and plays with the Peterborough Petes of the Ontario Hockey League. He plays for Team Canada in the World Junior Championships. Steve is selected fourth pick overall by the Detroit Red Wings in the 1983 NHL Entry Draft in Montreal.

1984 Ends his rookie season with the Wings as runner-up for the Calder Trophy (NHL's Rookie of the Year), a member of the NHL All-Rookie Team and voted top rookie by *The Sporting News*.

1986 Named captain at 21, youngest in Wings' history.

1987-93 Has six consecutive 100 point seasons, including career high 155 points and 65 goals for the 1988-89 season.

1997 Detroit Red Wings win Stanley Cup in four games over the Philadelphia Flyers; it is the team's first championship in 42 years.

1998 Represents Canada on Olympic team in Nagano. Wings win Stanley Cup second consecutive year in four games over the Washington Capitals; Yzerman awarded Conn Smythe Trophy as playoffs' Most Valuable Player.

1999 Signs contract that will make him a Detroit Red Wing for the remainder of his career.

Index

Further Reading

Fitzgerald, Francis J., editor. *Steve Yzerman: Heart of a Champion*. Louisville, Kentucky: Adcraft Sports Marketing Inc., 1996.

Harris, Paul. *Steve Yzerman: The Quiet Captain*. St. Louis, Missouri: GHB Publishers, 2000.

Resources

A to Z Encyclopedia of Ice Hockey.
www.azhockey.com

The Official Site of the National Hockey League.
www.nhl.com

Detroit Red Wings Official Team Site.
www.detroitredwings.com

Detroit Free Press.
www.freep.com

Photo Credits

DISNEYLAND'S HIDDEN MICKEYS

· · · · · · · · · · · · · · · · · · · ·

A Field Guide to
**Disneyland®
Resort's**
Best Kept Secrets

· · · · · · · · · · · · · · · · · · · ·

7th Edition

Steven M. Barrett

SMBBooks, Inc.

**DISNEYLAND'S
HIDDEN MICKEYS**
A Field Guide to Disneyland® Resort's
Best Kept Secrets
7th edition

by **Steven M. Barrett**

Published by
SMBBooks
7025 CR 46A, Suite 1071
Lake Mary, FL 32746
www.HiddenMickeyGuy.com

Trademarks, Etc. •••••••

Also by Steven M. Barrett

Hidden Mickeys:
A Field Guide to Walt Disney World's
Best Kept Secrets

Hidden Mickeys Go To Sea:
A Field Guide to the Disney Cruise Line's
Best Kept Secrets

Dedication • • • • • • • • • •

I dedicate this book to my wife Vickie and our son Steven, who support and help me with my Hidden Mickey passion, and to the many wonderful Hidden Mickey fans I've met through my website and in the Disney parks.

About the Author · · · · · ·

Author Steven M. Barrett paid his first
visit to Disneyland as a child. He has
hunted Hidden Mickeys at Disneyland
for years and wrote his first *Disneyland's Hidden Mickeys* book in 2007.
Because new Hidden Mickeys appear
over time and others are lost, he updates
the book every few years. In this book,
you'll find a Hidden Mickey Scavenger
Hunt for each of the theme parks, along
with a third hunt that includes Downtown Disney, the three resort hotels,
and other areas on Disneyland property.
To organize the Scavenger Hunts for
efficient touring, Steve consulted various guidebooks and conducted his own
research.

True to their name, Hidden Mickeys are elusive. New ones appear from time to time and some old ones disappear (see page 17). When that happens—and it will—I will let you know on my website:

www.HiddenMickeyGuy.com

So, if you can't find a Mickey—or if you're looking for just a few more—be sure to check out the website.

✳✳✳

Thank You, My Fellow Hidden Mickey Hunters

Scores of dedicated Mickey sleuths have helped me find the elusive Mouse. Many thanks to each and every one of you. You'll find your names in the *Acknowledgements*, beginning on page 155.

Table of Contents · · · · · ·

Maps

Read This First! · · · · · ·

My guess is that you have visited Disneyland before, perhaps many times. But if I've guessed wrong, and this is your first visit, then this note is for you.

Searching for Hidden Mickeys is lots of fun. But it's not a substitute for letting the magic of Disney sweep over you as you experience the Disneyland parks for the first time. For one thing, the scavenger hunts I present in this book do not include all the attractions in the Disneyland theme parks. That's because some of them don't have Hidden Mickeys! (Or their Hidden Mickeys are not visible to the general guest). Therefore, the first-time visitor should get ready for fun by also consulting a general Disneyland Resort guidebook for descriptions of Disneyland attractions, shows, dining, and other tourist information.

That doesn't mean you can't search for Hidden Mickeys, too. Just follow the suggestions in Chapter One of this book for *Finding Hidden Mickeys Without Scavenger Hunting.*

Chapter 1

#

Have you ever marveled at a "Hidden Mickey"? People in the know often shout with glee when they recognize one. Some folks are so involved with discovering them that Hidden Mickeys can be visualized where none actually exist. These outbreaks of Hidden Mickey mania are confusing to the unenlightened. So, let's get enlightened!

Here's the definition of an official Hidden Mickey: a partial or complete image of Mickey Mouse that has been hidden by Disney's lmagineers and artists in the designs of Disney attractions, hotels, restaurants, and other areas. These images are designed to blend into their surroundings. Sharp-eyed visitors have the fun of finding them.

The practice probably started as an inside joke among the lmagineers (the designers and builders of Disney attractions). According to Disney guru Jim Hill (JimHillMedia.com), Hidden Mickeys originated in the late 1970s or early 1980s, when Disney was building Epcot and management wanted to restrict Disney characters like Mickey and Minnie to Walt Disney World's Magic Kingdom. The lmagineers designing Epcot couldn't resist slipping Mickeys into the new park, and thus "Hidden Mickeys" were born. Guests and "Cast Members" (Disney employees) started spotting them and the concept took on a life of its own. Today, Hidden Mickeys are anticipated in any new Disney construction anywhere, and Hidden Mickey fans can't wait to find them.

Hidden Mickeys come in all sizes and many forms. The most common is an outline of Mickey's head formed by three intersecting circles, one for Mickey's round head and two for his round ears. Among Hidden Mickey fans, this image is known as the "classic" Hidden Mickey, a term I will adopt in this book. Other Hidden Mickeys include a side or oblique (usually three-quarter) profile of Mickey's face and head, a side profile of his entire body, a full-length silhouette of his body seen from the front, a detailed picture of his face or body, or a three-dimensional Mickey Mouse. Sometimes just his gloves, handprints, shoes, or ears appear. Even his name or initials in unusual places may qualify as a Hidden Mickey.

And it's not just Mickeys that are hidden. The term "Hidden Mickey" also applies to hidden images of other popular characters. There are Hidden Minnies, Hidden Donald Ducks, Hidden Goofys, and other Hidden Characters in the Disney theme parks, and I include many of them in this book.

The sport of finding Hidden Mickeys is catching on and adds even more interest to an already fun -filled Disneyland vacation. This book is your "field guide" to more than 420 Hidden Mickeys in the Disneyland Resort. To add to the fun, instead of just describing them, I've organized them into three scavenger hunts, one for each of the theme parks and one for all the rest of the Disneyland Resort: Downtown Disney District, the resort hotels, and beyond. The hunts are designed for maximum efficiency so that you can spend your time looking for Mickey rather than cooling your heels in lines. Follow the Clues and you will find the best Hidden Mickeys Disneyland has to offer. If you have trouble spotting a particular Hidden Mickey (some are extraordinarily well-camouflaged!), you can turn to the Hints at the end of each scavenger hunt for a fuller description.

Scavenger Hunting for Hidden Mickeys

To have the most fun and find the most Mickeys, follow these tips:

* **Arrive early** for the theme park hunts-45 minutes ahead of your entry time. If you're eligible for early entry (because you're holding a special ticket that allows early entry or you are staying in one of the three Disney Hotels and hold any valid park admission ticket), arrive at the early-entry park for that day 45 minutes or so before the early entry opening time. If you're not eligible for early entry, go to the non-early entry park for that day and arrive 45 minutes before the official opening time.

Choose a method to acquire FASTPASS-ES; either get them at FASTPASS distribution machines near the attractions that offer FASTPASSES, or download the free Disneyland app to your mobile device (you may want this app anyway as it provides other information you may find interesting), link your ticket to the app, and select FASTPASSES directly on the app (this option may cost you extra) once you've entered a park.

Pick up a Guidemap and Times Guide and plot your course. (A Times Guide is available at City Hall, or you can use your Disneyland app). Then look for

Hidden Mickeys in the waiting area while you wait for the rope to drop. You'll find the Clues for those areas by checking the Index to Mickey's Hiding Places in the back of this book. Look under "Entrance areas." You'll notice that headliner attractions are the first stops in the scavenger hunts. If you arrive later in the day, you may want to pick up a FASTPASS for the first major attraction and then skip down a few Clues to stay ahead of the crowd.

* **"Clues" and "Hints"**

Clues under each attraction will guide you to the Hidden Mickey(s). If you have trouble spotting them, you can turn to the Hints at the end of the hunt for a fuller description. The Clues and Hints are numbered consecutively, that is, Hint 1 goes with Clue 1, so it's easy to find the right Hint if you need it. In some cases, you may have to ride the attraction more than once to find all the Hidden Mickeys.

* **Scoring**

All Hidden Mickeys are fun to find, but all Hidden Mickeys aren't the same. Some are easier to find than others. I assign point values to Hidden Mickeys, identifying them as easy to spot (a value of 1 point) to difficult to find the first time (5 points). I also consider the complexity and uniqueness of the image: the more complex or unique the Hidden Mickey, the higher the point value. For example, some of the easy-to-spot Hidden Mickeys in Mickey's Toontown in Disneyland are one- or two-point Mickeys. The brilliantly camouflaged Mickey hiding in the tree on one of the ceramic panels decorating a column outside Disney's Grand Californian Hotel & Spa is a five-pointer (Clue 10 in the Downtown Disney and Hotel Scavenger Hunt).

* Playing the game

You can hunt solo or with others, just for fun or competitively. There's room to tally your score in the guide. Families with young children may want to focus on one- and two point Mickeys that the little ones will have no trouble spotting. (Of course, little ones tend to be sharp-eyed, so they may spot familiar shapes before you do in some of the more complex patterns.) Or you may want to split your party into teams and see who can rack up the most points (in which case, you'll probably want to have a copy of this guide for each team).

Of course, you don't have to play the game at all. You can simply look for Hidden Mickeys in attractions as you come to them. (See *Finding Hidden Mickeys Without Scavenger Hunting* below.)

* Following the Clues

The hunts often call for crisscrossing the parks. This may seem illogical at first, but trust me, it will keep you ahead of the crowd. Besides, it adds to the fun of the hunt and, if you're playing competitively, keeps everyone on their toes. Warning: Many Hidden Mickeys are waiting to be found in the Disney Parks. Depending on the crowds and the park hours when you visit, you may not be able to complete the Scavenger Hunt in one day!

* Waiting in line

Don't waste time in lines. If the wait is longer than 15 minutes, get a FASTPASS (if available and you're eligible), move on to the next attraction, and come back at your FASTPASS time. Exception: In some attractions, the Hidden Mickey(s) can only be seen from the standby (regular) queue line, and not from the

FASTPASS line. (I've not suggested FASTPASS in the Clues section when that is the case.) The lines at these attractions should not be too long if you start your scavenger hunt when the park opens and follow the hunt Clues as given. If you do encounter long lines, come back later during a parade or in the hour before the park closes. Alternatively, if you need to board an attraction with a long wait without a FASTPASS, use the Single Rider queue if available. (Check your Guidemap for a big "S" symbol next to the attraction.)

* Playing fair

Be considerate of other guests. Some Hidden Mickeys are in restaurants and shops. Ask a Cast Member's permission before searching inside sit-down restaurants and avoid the busy mealtime hours unless you are one of the diners. Tell the Cast Members and other guests who see you looking around what you're up to, so they can share in the fun.

Finding Hidden Mickeys Without Scavenger Hunting

If scavenger hunts don't appeal to you, you don't have to use them. You can find Hidden Mickeys in the specific rides and other attractions you visit by using the Index to Mickey's Hiding Places in the back of this book. Look up the attraction, restaurant, hotel, or shop in the Index, turn to the appropriate page in the book, and then follow the Clue(s) to find the Hidden Mickey(s).

Caution: You won't find every attraction, restaurant, hotel, or shop in the Index. Only those with confirmed Hidden Mickeys are included in this guide.

Hidden Mickeys: Real or Wishful Thinking?

The classic (three-circle) Mickeys are the most controversial, for good reason. Much debate surrounds the gathering of circular forms throughout Disneyland. The three cannonball craters in the wall of the fort in *Pirates of the Caribbean* (Clue 42 in the Disneyland Park Scavenger Hunt) is obviously the work of a clever artist. However, three-circle configurations occur spontaneously in art and nature, as in collections of grapes, tomatoes, pumpkins, bubbles, oranges, cannonballs, and the like. Unlike the cannonball crater Hidden Mickey in *Pirates of the Caribbean*, it may be difficult to attribute a random "classic Mickey" configuration of circles to a deliberate lmagineer design.

So which groupings of three circles qualify as Hidden Mickeys as opposed to wishful thinking? Unfortunately, no master list of actual or "lmagineer-approved" Hidden Mickeys exists. Purists demand that a true classic Hidden Mickey should have proper proportions and positioning. The round head must be larger than the ear circles (so that three equal circles in the proper alignment would not qualify as a Hidden Mickey). The head and ears must be touching and in perfect position for Mickey's head and ears.

On the other hand, Disney's mantra is: "If the guest thinks it's a Hidden Mickey, then by golly it is one!" Of course, I appreciate Disney's respect for their guests' opinions. However, when the subject is Hidden Mickeys, let's apply some guidelines. My own criteria are looser than the purist's but stricter than the "anything goes" Disney approach. I prefer to use a few sensible guidelines.

To be classified as a genuine classic Hidden Mickey, the three circles should satisfy the following criteria:

1. Purposeful (sometimes you can sense that the circles were placed on purpose).

2. Proportionate sizes (head larger than the ears and somewhat proportionate to the ears).

3. Round or at least "roundish."

4. The ears don't touch each other, and the ears are above the head (not beside it).

5. The head and ears touch or they're close to touching.

6. The grouping of circles is exceptional or unique in appearance.

7. The circles are hidden or somewhat hidden and not obviously decor (decorative).

Having spelled out some ground rules, allow me now to bend them in one instance. Some Hidden Mickeys are sentimental favorites with Disney fans, even though they may actually represent "wishful thinking." (My neighbor, Lew Brooks, calls them "two-beer" Mickeys.) Who am I to defy tradition? For example, the three circles on the back of the turtle in *Snow White's Scary Adventures* (Clue 146 in the Disneyland Park Scavenger Hunt) form a not-quite-proportionate "classic" Mickey. However, if you ask Cast Members near this attraction about a Hidden Mickey, they may whisper to you these cryptic words: "Watch for the turtle!"

Hidden Mickeys vs. Decorative Mickeys

Some Mickeys are truly hidden, not visible to the guest. They may be located behind the scenes, available only to Cast Members. You won't find them in this field guide, as I only include Hidden Mickeys that are accessible to the guest. Other Mickeys are decorative; they were placed in plain sight to enhance the decor. For example, in a restaurant, I consider a pat of butter shaped like Mickey Mouse to be a decorative (aka decor) Mickey. Disneyland is loaded with decorative Mickeys. You'll find obvious images of Mickey Mouse on items such as manhole covers, displays in shop windows, and restaurant menus. I do not include these ubiquitous and sometimes changing images in this book unless they are unique or hard to spot.

Hidden Mickeys can change or be accidentally (or purposefully) removed over time by the processes of nature or by the continual cleaning and refurbishing that goes on at Disneyland. For example, a classic Mickey on an Ace of Clubs card on the ceiling of the Main Street Magic Shop is no longer with us. Cast Members themselves sometimes create or remove Hidden Mickeys.

My Selection Process

I trust you've concluded by now that Hidden Mickey Science is an evolving specialty. Which raises the question: how did I choose the more than 420 Hidden Mickeys in the scavenger hunts in this guide? I compiled my list of Hidden Mickeys from all the resources to which

Disneyland's Hidden Mickeys

I had access: my own sightings, images sent to me by others (see "Acknowledgements," page 155), websites, books, and Cast Members. (Cast Members in each specific area usually -- but not always! -- know where some Hidden Mickeys are located.) Then I embarked on my verification hunts, asking for help along the way from generous Disney Cast Members. I have included only those Hidden Mickeys I could personally verify.

Furthermore, some Hidden Mickeys are visible only intermittently or only from certain vantage points in ride vehicles. I don't generally include these Mickeys, unless I feel that adequate descriptions will allow anyone to find them. So, the scavenger hunts include only those images I believe to be recognizable as Hidden Mickeys and visible to the general touring guest. It is quite likely, though, that one or more of the Hidden Mickeys described in this book will disappear over time.

If you find one missing before I do, I hope you'll let me know by sending a message to my website:

www.HiddenMickeyguy.com

I have enjoyed finding each and every Hidden Mickey in this book. I'm certain I'll find more as time goes by, and I hope you can spot new Hidden Mickeys during your visit. So, put on some comfortable walking shoes and experience the Disneyland Resort like you never have before! Enjoy the Hunt!

- Steve Barrett

Chapter 2

Disneyland Park Scavenger Hunt

*   Arrive at the entrance turnstiles (with your admission ticket) 45 minutes before the opening time for early entry (if you're eligible) or 45 minutes before official opening time if it's a non-early entry day.

Note: If Disneyland is crowded, it's more feasible to spread the Hidden Mickeys Scavenger Hunt over two days.

Clue 1: As soon as you pass through the entrance turnstiles, look around for a classic Mickey.
3 points

* Whenever you find yourself on Main Street, U.S.A., keep an eye out for the **Fire Engine**.

Clue 2: Check near the driver for a Hidden Mickey.
3 bonus points

* If it's an early-entry day, ride *Peter Pan's Flight*, then queue up at the rope at the Fantasyland entrance to Star Wars: Galaxy's Edge to ride *Millennium Falcon: Smugglers Run*.

If it's a non-early entry day, enter Star Wars: Galaxy's Edge to experience *Millennium Falcon: Smugglers Run*, and then ride *Peter Pan's Flight*.

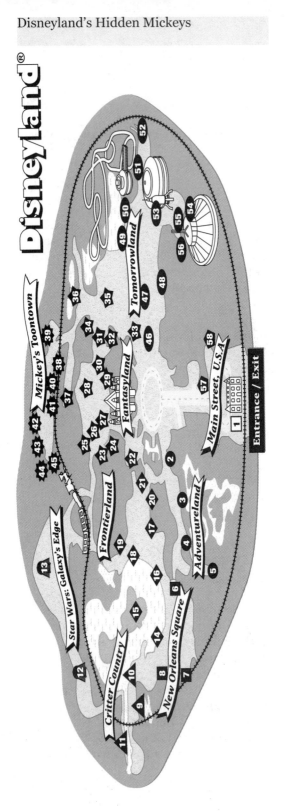

Disneyland®

1. Disneyland® Railroad, Entrance

 **Adventureland**
2. Walt Disney's Enchanted Tiki Room
3. Jungle Cruise
4. Tarzan's Treehouse™
5. Indiana Jones™ Adventure

■ **New Orleans Square**
6. Pirates of the Caribbean
7. Disneyland® Railroad
8. Haunted Mansion

Critter Country
9. Splash Mountain
10. Davy Crockett's Explorer Canoes
11. The Many Adventures of Winnie the Pooh

Star Wars: Galaxy's Edge
12. Star Wars: Rise of the Resistance
13. Millennium Falcon: Smugglers Run

◆ **Frontierland**
14. Raft to Tom Sawyer Island
15. Pirate's Lair on Tom Sawyer Island
16. Fantasmic!
17. The Golden Horseshoe Stage
18. Mark Twain Riverboat and Sailing Ship Columbia
19. Big Thunder Mountain Railroad
20. Pioneer Mercantile shop
21. Frontierland Shootin' Exposition

◆ **Fantasyland**
22. Fantasy Faire
23. Pinocchio's Daring Journey
24. Snow White's Scary Adventures
25. Casey Jr. Circus Train
26. King Arthur Carrousel
27. Sleeping Beauty Castle Walkthrough
28. Dumbo the Flying Elephant
29. Peter Pan's Flight
30. Mr. Toad's Wild Ride
31. Mad Tea Party
32. Alice in Wonderland
33. Pixie Hollow
34. Storybook Land Canal Boats
35. Matterhorn Bobsleds
36. "it's a small world"
37. Fantasyland Theatre

✷ **Mickey's Toontown**
38. Disneyland® Railroad
39. Roger Rabbit's Car Toon Spin
40. Goofy's Playhouse
41. Donald's Boat
42. Minnie's House
43. Mickey's House
44. Chip 'n Dale Treehouse
45. Gadget's Go Coaster

● **Tomorrowland**
46. Astro Orbitor
47. Buzz Lightyear Astro Blasters
48. Star Tours – The Adventures Continue
49. Finding Nemo Submarine Voyage
50. Disneyland® Monorail
51. Autopia
52. Disneyland® Railroad
53. Star Wars Launch Bay
54. Space Mountain
55. Tomorrowland Theater
56. Starcade

⬠ **Main Street, U.S.A.**
57. Main Street Cinema
58. The Disneyland® Story … Mr. Lincoln

21

*
Ride *Millennium Falcon: Smugglers Run*

Clue 3: Look around the briefing room (just before you enter the cockpit) for a classic Hidden Mickey.
3 points

Clue 4: When you're seated in the cockpit, search the ceiling for a Hidden Mickey.
3 points

Clue 5: Stroll around the area near the entrance to *Millennium Falcon Smuggler's Run* for a Hidden Mickey on an outside wall.
4 points

Clue 6: Explore the middle entrance to Star Wars: Galaxy's Edge (the entrance across from *Big Thunder Mountain Railroad*) and search a rock wall near the bridge for a Hidden Mickey.
5 points

Clue 7: While you're near the bridge at this middle entrance, look up for a rock shaped like Donald Duck.
4 points

*
Ride *Peter Pan's Flight*

Clue 8: Study the handrail posts near the loading dock for a Hidden Mickey.
4 points

Clue 9: At the beginning of the ride, read two names in blocks below you.
4 points for finding both

Clue 10: Look for Mickey in Big Ben.
5 points

*
Outside *Peter Pan's Flight* ...

22

Clue 11: Search high for a Hidden Mickey.
 3 points

* Then walk toward the **Matterhorn Bobsleds** in Fantasyland. Observe the side of the mountain that faces "it's a small world."

Clue 12: Locate a Mickey clearing in the snow.
5 points

* Line up for the Bobsleds ride in the right hand queue.

Clue 13: Study the right Bobsleds queue area for a Hidden Mickey on a coat of arms.
4 points

Clue 14: While on the ride, stay alert for a Hidden Mickey in an ice cave.
5 bonus points

Clue 15: Walk to a small alcove on the Tomorrowland side of the Matterhorn and find Nemo!
4 points

Clue 16: Stroll toward Tomorrowland and search for a Mickey-shaped hole on the outside of Matterhorn Mountain.
4 points

* Get a FASTPASS for *Space Mountain* for later. (Keep track of your FASTPASS time window!)

* Line up at the **Pixie Hollow** meet and greet area.

Clue 17: At the end of the waiting queue, don't overlook a classic Mickey.
4 points

23

*
   Head next to **Buzz Lightyear Astro Blasters** in Tomorrowland.

Clue 18: Search for two Mickey continents along the entrance queue.
6 points for finding both

Clue 19: Find two classic (three-circle) Hidden Mickeys along the entrance queue.
6 points for finding both

Clue 20: Now spot an oblong satellite on the wall with a Hidden Mickey on its side.
4 points

Clue 21: On the ride, watch to your left for a classic Mickey on a block.
3 points

Clue 22: After you step off the ride vehicle, search for a side-profile Mickey on the wall.
2 points

Clue 23: Find two classic Mickeys in the same area.
2 points each

*
   Get in line for **Gadget 's Go Coaster**. The Hidden Mickeys here are along the queue. You can skip the actual ride if you want; just ask to exit when you reach the loading area.

Clue 24: Stay alert for at least three rock classic Mickeys in the queue walls.
3 points each; 9 points total

Clue 25: Gaze around the vehicle loading area for a Hidden Mickey.
4 points

* Check into **Star Tours-The Adventures Continue**.

Clue 26: Along the entrance queue, spot a Hidden Mickey near C-3PO.
3 points

Clue 27: Now wait for a shadow Hidden Mickey in a video on a wall display along the entrance queue.
4 points

Clue 28: Stay alert for another shadow Mickey image on the wall to your right along the entrance queue.
5 points

Clue 29: Next, study the entrance queue luggage scanner for Mickey and other Disney characters and images.
5 points total for finding Mickey and two or more other Disney images

Clue 30: After you're seated in the ride vehicle, C-3PO appears on a screen to your right. Scan him for a Hidden Mickey.
5 points

Clue 31: At the end of the ride, if you dive down to the Coruscant planet (as opposed to other random end destinations for the ride), don't miss three faint blue circles that form a large classic Mickey on the right side of the screen.
5 bonus points

Clue 32: As your vehicle continues down to Coruscant and crash lands on a platform, look for classic Mickeys on a rear wall.
5 bonus points

* Return to **Space Mountain** during your FASTPASS window and walk up the entrance queue. You can skip the ride if you want; there were no Hidden Mickeys in it last time I checked.

Clue 33: See anything on the ride vehicles?
2 points

*
Get a FASTPASS for *Fantasmic!* at a kiosk along the Rivers of America (usually near *Mark Twain Riverboat* landing). Also get a FASTPASS for *IndianaJones Adventure*.

*
Get in line for **Mr. Toad's Wild Ride**.
Clue 34: Find a tiny Mickey
along the inside entrance queue.
4 points

Clue 35: At the beginning of the ride, stare at a right-hand door for a tiny dark Mickey in the door's stained glass.
5 points

Clue 36: Search for Mickey in beer foam.
4 points

Clue 37: Stay alert for Sherlock Holmes in a window. (A Hidden Surprise, not a Hidden Mickey!)
5 points

*
Wander over to New Orleans Square and hop on **Pirates of the Caribbean**.

Clue 38: During the first part of your boat ride, study the water for Mickey.
5 points

Clue 39: Stay alert for Mickey on a chair by a bed.
4 points

Clue 40: After you pass the skeleton in bed, look back for an image of Goofy.
5 points

Clue 41: In the first fight scene with the pirate ship firing cannonballs, watch a window in a building for Mickey.
5 points

Clue 42: In the first fight scene, spot a classic Mickey on a wall.
5 points

Clue 43: Stare at the wall behind the cats by the drunken pirate. See a classic Mickey?
4 points

Clue 44: Near the end of the ride, study the armor on the wall for a classic Mickey.
5 points

Clue 45: Find a classic Mickey on a chair in Jack Sparrow's treasure room.
4 points

Clue 46: After you exit the boat, look around for a classic Mickey on a door.
2 points

Clue 47: Study the outside railings in New Orleans Square for some famous initials (another Hidden Surprise).
5 points for both names

*
Turn left at the exit to enjoy **Haunted Mansion**.

Clue 48: Look high along the mansion walls inside for a Hidden Mickey.
3 points

Clue 49: Search for Mickey in the wallpaper.
3 points

Clue 50: While on the ride, can you find Donald Duck?
4 points

Clue 51: Study a floating table for a Hidden Mickey.
4 points

Clue 52: If snow is in the ballroom, find Mickey!
5 points

Clue 53: As you ride, keep alert for plates and saucers.
3 points

Clue 54: In the attic, look for a clock with a Hidden Mickey.
5 points

*
   Mosey on over to **The Golden Horseshoe** in Frontierland. You can order a counter-service meal and, if the timing is right, catch a great show on its stage (check your Times Guide or Disneyland app for show times, and while you're at it, plan to enjoy a 2:30 p.m. or later showing of *Mickey and the Magical Map*).

Clue 55: Check around the stage for a classic Mickey.
3 points

Clue 56: Now study the wall paintings for a Hidden Mickey.
3 points

*
Walk to Adventureland during your next FASTPASS window and enjoy **Indiana Jones Adventure**.

Clue 57: Stay alert for a Hidden Mickey made of pearls on the wall of the inside queue.
4 points

28

Clue 58: Study the walls of the stand-by queue for Mickey's "initials."
4 points

Clue 59: In the circular room with the rope you can pull on, search for a stone slab (propped upright) with a tiny classic Mickey. (Note: This image is becoming more faint with time and may disappear.)
5 points

Clue 60: Now look up for another classic Mickey in the same room.
3 points

Clue 61: Find a large classic Mickey in the room with the video screen.
3 points

Clue 62: Toward the end of the video room, look up and say "hi" to Eeyore!
4 points

Clue 63: When you leave the video room, peer into an office to spot Mickey (and/or Minnie).
3 points

Clue 64: After the ride starts, gaze up into Mara's huge face for a classic Mickey.
3 points

Clue 65: When your vehicle enters the Mummy Room, find a Mickey Mouse hat.
5 points

*
Get a FASTPASS for *Splash Mountain* to ride later.

*
Hop on the **Disneyland Railroad** train at the New Orleans Square station and ride around the park. You can exit at New Orleans Square station and walk to

29

your next destination.

Clue 66: Now keep your eyes peeled for a Hidden Mickey in grapes.
3 points

*
Ride **Mark Twain Riverboat** or **Sailing Ship Columbia**.

Clue 67: Study a bridge for a classic Hidden Mickey washer under a bolt.
5 points

Clue 68: Squint for a Hidden Mickey hole under the bridge.
5 points

Clue 69: Seek out the *Mark Twain Riverboat* (if you haven't already). Concentrate on the front of the ship to spot a Hidden Mickey.
2 points

Clue 70: Search for Mickey Mouse in a painting near the *Mark Twain Riverboat* loading dock.
5 points

*
Float on the Raft to **Tom Sawyer Island**.
Clue 71: On *Tom Sawyer Island*, seek out a cavern entrance with a classic Mickey.
3 points

Clue 72: Look for two Hidden Mickey locks in a cave.
3 points

Clue 73: Study the treasure in the *Pirate 's Lair* for a classic Mickey.
4 points

*
Return by raft to Frontierland. Ride **Splash Mountain** during your FASTPASS window.

Clue 74: Check out the outside entrance queue for a tiny Mickey.
5 points

Clue 75: Search for a classic Mickey along the inside queue.
3 points

Clue 76: Look up for Mickey just before the big drop.
4 points

*
Get a FASTPASS for *Big Thunder Mountain Railroad*.

*
Walk to Tomorrowland. Go to **Finding Nemo Submarine Voyage** and then look for the *Monorail* exit to find the elevator for the **Disneyland Monorail**.

Clue 77: First go up to the *Monorail* exit deck to spot a Hidden Mickey near the water below you. (Note: This Hidden Mickey comes and goes.)
4 bonus points

Clue 78: Now search for Mickey near the elevator on the ground level.
5 points

Ask a Cast Member for permission to enter the **Marine Observation Outpost** at the right side of the *Finding Nemo Submarine Voyage* entrance queue.

Clue 79: Look around inside for a Hidden Mickey.
4 points

*
Walk along the entrance queue for *Autopia*.
Clue 80: Find a classic Mickey on the cars.
3 points

*
Make time in your schedule for the
afternoon parade. (Note: The parade floats change from time to time
but usually include Hidden Mickeys in
their decoration.) The antique Grand
Marshal automobile sometimes leads
the parade.

Clue 81: Search this antique car for
several Hidden Mickeys.
5 bonus points for finding three or more

*
Walk to the *Fantasyland Theatre*
at your chosen time for a showing of
Mickey and the Magical Map.

Clue 82: Scan the overhead stage
border. You might find Mickey!
3 points

Clue 83: Study the left side of the
stage for a classic Mickey in a window.
4 points

Clue 84: During the show, spot a
classic Mickey at the right rear of the
stage.
3 points

Clue 85: Keep looking for Mickey
inside some bubbles!
4 points

Clue 86: Stay alert for a classic Mickey
that floats up the rear screen.
3 points

Clue 87: Watch the show as a black
splotch turns into a classic Mickey,
just for a second.
5 points

*
Cross Fantasyland to **Fantasy Faire**.
Clue 88: Search for a classic Hidden
Mickey inside the Music Box.
5 points

Clue 89: Now scan the crowd inside the Music Box for Disney Characters.
5 points for five or more

*
Walk to **Big Thunder Mountain Railroad** in Frontierland during your FASTPASS window.

Clue 90: Look for a Hidden Mickey on a sign outside the attraction.
4 points

Clue 91: While on the ride, search for three gears that form a classic Mickey.
3 points

Clue 92: Find Mickey at the exit.
3 points

*
Now return to Adventureland and hop on **Jungle Cruise**.

Clue 93: Glance up outside the entrance for a Hidden Character.
2 points

Clue 94: In the last part of the entrance queue, stay vigilant for a Hidden Mickey inside a bag in a caged display. It's best seen from the right-side queue.
3 points

Clue 95: On the boat ride, check out the gorilla camp scene for a Hidden Mickey on the ground.
4 points

Clue 96: From your boat, look behind the dancing and chanting natives for a *Lion King* image. (This isn't a Hidden Mickey; it's a cool Hidden Surprise!)
5 points

Clue 97: Search the side of the river for Donald Duck's face on a native.
4 points

*
If you're up for a mild climb through an imaginative tree, check out **Tarzan's Treehouse** in Adventureland.

Clue 98: Study the room with the ship's wheel for a Hidden Mickey on the wall.
3 points

Clue 99: Along your walk through the tree, two characters from Beauty and the Beast make an appearance.
4 points for finding both

*
Stop by Bengal Barbecue or Royal Street Veranda for dinner. Be aware of your FASTPASS time for *Fantasmic!* and the time for the *Fireworks* show.

*
Stroll toward **Walt Disney's Enchanted Tiki Room**.

Clue 100: Observe the shields outside near the exit to find a classic Mickey.
3 points

*
Walk to Mickey's Toontown
(Note: You'll find many Mickey shapes throughout Toontown. I don't include the larger, more obvious Mickey images as Hidden Mickeys; they're more properly designated decor Mickeys.)

Clue 101: Look for Mickey near the entrance to Mickey's Toontown.
2 points

*
Saunter over to **Minnie's House**.

Clue 102: Mickey is hiding in Minnie's kitchen.
2 points

Search for Mickey outside Minnie's House.

Clue 103: Look near and to the right of the big blue doors for a classic Hidden Mickey.
3 points

Clue 104: Now look above and behind the big blue doors for a Hidden Surprise!
5 points

*
Stroll over to **Mickey's House**.
Clue 105: See anything in his front door?
1 point

Clue 106: Glance down for Mickey.
1 point

Clues 107 and 108: Look inside a glass-fronted bookcase for some Hidden Mickeys.
3 points total for finding one on each of two books

Clue 109: Stare at other books in the first room.
3 points

Clues 110 and 111: In the piano room, search for two Hidden Mickeys in a bookcase.
2 points each; 4 points total

Clue 112: Find classic Mickeys and another Hidden Character in the piano.
5 points for a Hidden Mickey and another character

Clue 113: Something's atop the piano.
2 points

Clue 114: Look for Mickey on a drum.
2 points

Clue 115: Spot Mickey on a clock.
2 points

Clue 116: Pay attention to a special mirror inside *Mickey's Movie Barn* (the room in Mickey's House where you wait to meet Mickey in person).
4 points

Clue 117: Study Donald's workbench for a paint-splotch Hidden Mickey.
3 points

Clue 118: Also, in *Mickey's Movie Barn*, watch the countdown screen.
3 points

Clue 119: Once outside, admire Mickey's car and find Hidden Mickeys.
3 points for one or more

Clue 120: Search for Mickey on a lamp.
3 points

*
   If you're in Mickey's Toontown when **Clarabelle's Snack Stand** closes, look around for a Hidden Mickey. (Ask a Cast Member when *Clarabelle's* will close; you may need to return later.)

Clue 121: At closing, a Hidden Mickey appears.
2 points

Clue 122: Find two more at the **Post Office**.
4 points for finding both

Clue 123: Ring the doorbell at the **Toontown Fire Department** and watch for a Hidden Mickey.
4 points

Clue 124: Study the roof of the **Fireworks Factory** for a small, blue classic Mickey.
5 points

Clue 125: Do you see a tiny Hidden Mickey in front of **Goofy's Playhouse**?
3 points

* Now stroll over to **The Many Adventures of Winnie the Pooh** in Critter Country.

Clue 126: Study the "Hunny Pot" vehicles for a classic Mickey.
2 points

Clue 127: Just after the ride starts, be aware of a classic Mickey in the wood.
5 points

Clue 128: After the Heffalumps and Woozles dream room, search high behind you for a Hidden Surprise. (It's not a Hidden Mickey, but it's a cool image that everyone should enjoy.)
5 points

Clue 129: Look for classic Mickey circles near Heffalumps.
3 points

Visit **Pooh Corner** store nearby.

Clue 130: Discover a Hidden Surprise inside the store: two references to the Country Bear Jamboree - a previous attraction near this site.
4 points

Walk to the **Briar Patch** store in Critter Country (near *Splash Mountain*).

Clue 131: Look inside the store for a Hidden Mickey on a shelf.
3 points

*
  Queue up to ride *Alice in Wonderland*.

Clue 132: In the first part of the ride, watch for a small house (the White Rabbit's house) for a Hidden Mickey inside the open window.
5 points

Clue 133: On the ride, search for a classic Mickey in red paint.
4 points

*
Walk to the *Storybook Land Canal Boats* ride and study the boats before you board and after you exit your boat.

Clue 134: A Hidden Mickey is on the back of the "Daisy" boat.
3 points

Clue 135: Study the "Flora" boat for a Hidden Mickey.
4 points

Clue 136: A bluebird on the back of the "Snow White" boat is looking at this Hidden Mickey.
5 points

Clue 137: Don't forget the "Wendy" boat's Hidden Mickey!
2 points

Clue 138: On the boat ride, squint for a tiny classic Mickey on a building in Pinocchio's Village, just after Monstro the Whale.
5 points

Clue 139: While on the boat ride, search for a Hidden Mickey above a village.
3 points

*
Go to **Pinocchio's Daring Journey**
in Fantasyland.

Clue 140: Scan the loading dock area for
a Hidden Mickey in front of a blue door.
3 points

Clue 141: Watch the floor to spot a yellow Hidden Mickey.
4 points

Clue 142: Check the popcorn stand on
your right for a classic Mickey.
4 points

Clue 143: Spot a Hidden Mickey under
a glass globe with a fish.
4 points

Clue 144: Look for a Hidden Mickey
near a ship.
5 points

*
Step over to **Snow White 's Scary
Adventures**.

Clue 145: Find Mickey at the loading dock.
3 points

Clue 146: On the ride, watch for a
classic Mickey on an animal.
3 points

Clue 147: Check out a Hidden Tinker
Bell near a mine car full of jewels.
5 points

*
Relax on a gentle boat ride at **"it's a
small world."**

Clue 148: Look for Mickey along the
entrance queue.
3 points

Clue 149: Stay alert for Hidden Characters.
5 points for spotting five or more

Clue 150: Study a balloon above you for a Hidden Mickey bear shadow.
4 points

Clue 151: Keep your eyes peeled for a bear's head that looks like Mickey's head.
3 points

Clue 152: Near the end of the ride, watch the ceiling for a Hidden Mickey.
4 points

*
Stroll over to **King Arthur Carrousel**. Find the Hidden Mickeys from outside the carrousel.

Clue 153: Check out the horses in the outer circle for Hidden Mickeys.
2 points each; 4 points total

*
Cross Fantasyland to the **Mad Hatter shop**, not far from the *Mad Tea Party* attraction.

Clue 154: Search around inside the shop for a Hidden cat.
5 points

Clue 155: Spot Hidden Mickeys outside the shop.
2 points each for two Hidden Mickeys

*
Back near *Sleeping Beauty Castle*, locate the **Castle Heraldry Shoppe**.

Clue 156: Find two Hidden Mickeys outside the store.
5 points for finding both

*
Retrace your steps to **The Star Trader** shop (not far from *Star Tours*).

Clue 157: Glance inside *The Star Trader* for small classic Mickeys in poles. (You can spot this image in other Disney stores as well).
2 points

Clue 158: Now find two different Hidden Mickeys on merchandise bins. (You can spot these images in other Disney stores as well).
3 points for finding both types

*
Step over to the **Little Green Men Store Command** (next to *Buzz Lightyear Astro Blasters*).

Clue 159: Look for Mickey on a sign.
4 points

*
Walk toward the central hub.

Clue 160: Study the spheres of the **Astro Orbitor**.
2 points

*
Cross the central hub to the walkway to Frontierland.

Clue 161: Look for a Hidden Mickey along the entrance walkway to Frontierland.
3 points

*
Stop in at the **Frontierland Shootin' Exposition**.

Clue 162: Spot a Hidden Mickey toward the front of the shootin' area.
3 points

*Enter the **Pioneer Mercantile** shop.

Clue 163: Examine the wall for Mickey.
3 points

*Walk to the **Rancho del Zocalo Restaurante**.

Clue 164: Search inside the restaurant for a classic Mickey in wood.
4 points

*Return to Main Street, U.S.A.

Clue 165: Check a painting inside the **Plaza Inn Restaurant**.
3 points

*Enter the **Photo Supply Company**.

Clue 166: Look for Mickey on a camera.
3 points

*Stand outside the **Silhouette Studio**.

Clue 167: Spot a Hidden Mickey in a display window.
4 points

Clue 168: Find a Hidden Mickey outside on a **fruit cart**.
4 points

*Stroll down Main Street to **Main Street Cinema**. Walk inside.

Clue 169: Look around for some Hidden Mickeys.
3 points for one or more

Clue 170: Outside *Main Street Cinema*, search for two Hidden Mickeys.
2 points each; 4 points total

* Find more Mickeys at the **Main Street Magic Shop**.

Clue 171: Spot Mickey on a display shelf.
3 points

Clue 172: Locate a classic Mickey outside the shop.
3 points

* Walk toward the Castle to the **Penny Arcade**.

Clue 173: Don't miss the small Hidden Mickey on a game machine inside the *Penny Arcade*!
4 points

* Approach the **Gibson Girl Ice Cream Parlor**.

Clue 174: Admire the outside windows for a Hidden Mickey.
4 points

* Stroll to the **Emporium** store.

Clue 175: Inside an entrance at the end of the store closest to *City Hall*, search for Mickey in a painting on the wall.
5 points

Clue 176: Find a room in the store with toy merchandise and look for a train circling a track overhead. Wait for a lighted Hidden Mickey to appear!
5 points

* Cross Main Street to the **Mad Hatter**.

Clue 177: Scan all the windows outside the store for a Hidden Mickey.
5 points

*
Walk to the Main Street Station of the
Disneyland Railroad.

Clue 178: Wait for the trains and
study their forward sections for
Hidden Mickeys.
5 points total for one or more

*
Watch the ***Fantasmic!*** show for Hidden Mickeys.

Clue 179: Be alert for a Hidden Mickey in white foam on the water screen.
5 points

Clue 180: Study a mirror for a Hidden
Mickey.
4 points

*
Don't miss the nighttime ***fireworks***
show!

Clue 181: Watch the sky during the
fireworks show for a Hidden Mickey.
5 bonus points

*
Exit Disneyland Park.
Clue 182: In the ***entrance plaza***, look
for Mickey at your feet.
3 points

Clue 183: Spot Mickey at the tops and
bottoms of some of the poles.
4 points for spotting Mickey in both
places

Now total your score and see how you
did.

Total Points for Disneyland Park =

How'd You Do?

Up to 267 points - Bronze
268 to 534 points - Silver
535 points and over - Gold
667 points - Perfect Score

(If you earned bonus points by spotting Hidden Mickeys in the *Main Street Fire Engine*, the *Matterhorn Bobsleds'* ice cave, *Star Tours*, the boat docks at *Finding Nemo Submarine Voyage*, on the Grand Marshal's car during the *afternoon parade*, or during the evening *fireworks* show, you may have done even better.)

Notes

If you need help, the Hints are here for you!

Entrance

Hint 1: As soon as you enter Disney-land, turn around and spot the classic Mickey speaker grid on the utility box next to the entrance turnstile. (Note: The ticket attendant may be blocking your view.)

Hint 2: Whenever you walk down Main Street, U.S.A., look for the *Fire Engine*. In front of the driver, the key chain hanging from the ignition key is often the smiling face of Mickey Mouse.

Star Wars: Galaxy's Edge

- *Millennium Falcon: Smuggler's Run*

Hint 3: A sideways classic Hidden Mickey made of round silver metal wheels sits on one side of the wall video monitor.

Hint 4: On the middle front of the cockpit ceiling, a small metal classic Mickey is visible between two small flexible pipes.

Hint 5: On a wall near the entrance to *Millennium Falcon: Smugglers Run*, blast marks come together as a classic Hidden Mickey. To find the wall, go up the stairs or ramp to the left of the entrance to Millennium Falcon (as you face it). The Hidden Mickey is on a side wall, about five feet above the walkway.

Hint 6: Walk from Frontierland along the middle entrance to Star Wars: Galaxy's Edge. Pass under the bridge and scan the rock wall to your left. About 15 feet or so past the bridge, you'll spot a small, faint, dark classic Mickey marking a few inches above the walkway.

Hint 7: Now walk back toward the bridge and look up. A rock shaped like Donald Duck is perched next to and above the left side of the bridge. You'll see the side view of Donald's head silhouetted against the sky.

Fantasyland

- *Peter Pan's Flight*

Hint 8: When you reach the section of the entrance queue that's alongside the loading dock area, find the seventh handrail post from the end of the handrail to your right. Midway up the post, an upright classic Hidden Mickey design faces you.

Hint 9: As you walk through the entrance queue, lean over the rail and look into the first scene (the bedroom) of the ride. Alphabet blocks are stacked and scattered on the floor. On the ride, as your vehicle soars over the bedroom, look down at the blocks and find these words: "DISNEY" (spelled as "Dl3NEY") and "PETER PAN." (Cast Members sometimes change these blocks around.)

Hint 10: As you fly over London, a side-view Mickey silhouette hides in a top window on the left side of Big Ben. Look back at the window as you pass by the clock tower.

Hint 11: Inside a high window to the left of the entrance to the attraction, classic Mickeys are on the bottom of a plush bear's paws. The paws are at the lower right, next to the window curtain.

- Matterhorn Bobsleds

Hint 12: Admire the Matterhorn from in front of Le Petit Chalet shop near *"it's a small world."* About two -thirds the way up the side of the mountain, a clearing in the snow forms a classic Mickey, tilted to the left.

Hint 13: A tiny black classic Mickey is in the middle of a red and white coat of arms at the rear of the right queue. The Mickey is on a red triangle at the bottom of a white pole.

Hint 14: To your left during the first part of the ride, on the floor of the first ice cave, where you will see expedition equipment and glowing crystals, a rope between the ice crystals and the crates is coiled into a classic Mickey. (Note: This Hidden Mickey comes and goes.)

Hint 15: Exit *Matterhorn Bobsleds* on the Tomorrowland side to find a Hidden Nemo traced on the side of a wooden electrical box. It's across the walkway from the Matterhorn exit at an entrance to a small alcove.

- *view of Matterhorn Mountain*

Hint 16: A large black classic Mickey hole hides in the side of the Matterhorn Mountain. You can see it from various vantage points in Tomorrowland.

- *Pixie Hollow*

Hint 17: At the end of the *Pixie Hollow* waiting queue is a signpost that reads "Fairies Welcome." A classic Mickey is carved out of bark on the front of the signpost, near the bottom.

Tomorrowland

- *Buzz Lightyear Astro Blasters*

Hint 18: As soon as you enter the building, look for two "Ska-densii" planets with side profile "continent" Mickeys along the right-side wall.

Hint 19: Two upside-down classic Mickeys appear in the large "Planets of the Galactic Alliance" mural on the wall of the entrance queue. One is located at about the "10 o'clock" position in the planet named K'lifooel'ch; it is made of small green spheres. The other is made of white spheres and hides on the right side of the mural above the words "K'tleendon Kan Cluster."

Hint 20: Watch the wall for an oblong satellite (called "Green Planet" on the queue mural) with an antenna on top and green swirls on the side. Three swirls in the middle of its side form a tilted classic Hidden Mickey. This planet appears on the wall several times during the ride.

Hint 21: A classic Mickey is etched on a block in the first show room to the left of the vehicle, just past a large rotating wheel and left of a row of target batteries.

Hint 22: A side-profile Mickey hides on a "Ska-densii" planet's continent on a right wall mural across from the photo-viewing area. If it looks familiar, it's because you see the same Hidden Mickeys (as well as the two below) on an entrance-queue mural.

Hint 23: On this same mural on the right wall along the inside exit, look for K'lifooel'ch, the planet formed of many small green spheres. A classic Mickey lies along the outer edge of K'lifooel'ch at about the "10 o'clock" location (other classic Mickey spheres are also part of this planet), and an upside-down classic Mickey is formed by three white spheres at the middle right of the mural, above the words "K'tleendon Kan Cluster."

Mickey's Toontown

- Gadget's Go Coaster

Hint 24: The following three classic

Mickeys aren't perfectly proportional, but they seem purposeful:
- The first is at the first turn to the left in the entrance queue.
- The second is across from a bonsai tree and before the last right turn.
- The third is a somewhat distorted classic Mickey, tilted sideways, at the end of the wall on the left and about 20 feet before the boarding area.

Hint 25: Inside the loading area, turn around and locate the only blueprint on the rear wall. A partial drawing of Mickey Mouse is on the right side of the blueprint. Under Mickey are the words "DOG & PONY FOR MICKEY AT 4 PM."

Tomorrowland

- Star Tours-The Adventures Continue

Hint 26: Circles create a Mickey hat with ears on the upper part of the control panel behind C-3 PO ' s head.

Hint 27: In a wall display along the entrance queue, the silhouette of R2-D2 appears several times in a continuous video loop of moving shadow figures. At one point, R2-D2 sprouts satellite ears that rotate into round "Mickey ears" for a few seconds.

Hint 28: Along the right side of the entrance queue ramps, in the second room with the luggage inspection, a small droid casts a shadow of Mickey ears on the wall.

Hint 29: Along the entrance queue, a robot watches a continuous scan of luggage moving along a conveyor belt. You can spot images of a plush Mickey

Mouse and a plush Goofy, along with images of Buzz Lightyear, Aladdin's lamp, a Sorcerer Mickey hat, a Mr. Incredible shirt, Madame Leota's crystal ball, and others.

Hint 30: Just after you're seated, C-3PO appears in a screen at the front right of the room. A small, bright white classic Mickey is on his right forearm near his wrist.

Hint 31: Coruscant is one of three different and random end destinations for your *Star Tours* journey. As you dive down to the planet and fly among the buildings, stare at the lower right side of the video screen. Three large, faint blue translucent circles come together as a classic Hidden Mickey!

Hint 32: Four more classic Hidden Mickeys can be spotted in the Coruscant landing sequence. After your *Star Tours* vehicle crash lands on a platform and is lowered below into a hanger, look for four recessed panels in the top half of the back wall of the hanger. A classic Mickey is in the center of each panel. To see them, focus on the background wall instead of the droid in the foreground that's flying around with the two light batons.

- Space Mountain

Hint 33: The speakers on the back of the ride-vehicle seats form classic Mickeys.

Fantasyland

- Mr. Toad's Wild Ride

Hint 34: On the large statue of Mr. Toad, to the left of the inside entrance queue, tiny red splotches can be seen in the lower part of both corneas (above the white part of the eyes). Both splotches resemble classic Hidden Mickeys, but the one in Mr. Toad's left eye (as you face the statue, it's the eye on the right) is more convincing.

Hint 35: At the beginning of the ride, on the third set of doors that your car drives through, you'll see the head and ears of a tiny dark Mickey. It's in the right door's lower left panel, in the bottom left-most triangle of stained glass. It's hard to spot!

Hint 36: In Winky's Pub, about halfway through the ride, an upside-down classic Mickey appears in the foam in the top left corner of the left mug (as you face the scene) above Winky's hand.

Hint 37: The silhouette of Sherlock Holmes can be found on the second-floor window above the Constabulary door. It's in the city room (the room with the fountain) just after you pass the bartender who spins the mugs. Once you leave the pub room, look directly to the left and up a little and you'll see Sherlock. (He's not a Disney character, but this is one cool hidden image nonetheless.)

New Orleans Square

- Pirates of the Caribbean

Hint 38: As you drift past the Blue Bayou Restaurant seating area, a classic Mickey appears in the water to the right of your boat. It's formed by the last set of three lily pads that you pass before you enter the caverns.

Hint 39: To the left of your boat, a classic Mickey hides on the upper back of the chair to the right of the bed where the pirate skeleton is lying.

Hint 40: Just after you float by the skeleton in bed on your left, look back at the ceiling of the cavern behind you for a large rock that juts out over the water above you. The shape of the rock resembles Goofy.

Hint 41: When you enter the battle scene with the pirate ship firing cannonballs, watch the window above and in front of you with the fighting silhouettes. At several points during the scuffle, you can spot an outline of Mickey's head and ears.

Hint 42: In the battle scene with the pirate ship firing cannonballs, there are three cannonball impact craters on the upper part of the fort wall on the right side of your boat. This crater classic Mickey is below the middle fort cannon and best seen if you turn around to view it as you are passing by the fort.

Hint 43: Stay alert for the cats to the right of the drunken pirate sitting on a barrel. A shadow on the wall behind the cats forms a classic Mickey at times.

Hint 44: This classic Mickey is to the left of your boat in the last room, where pieces of armor hang from the wall. Look for the gold breastplate, often the leftmost armor breastplate, with a coat of arms emblem. In the center of that emblem are classic Mickey circles. (Note: The items in the armor display are moved around at times.)

Hint 45: In the last treasure room to your left, three circles at the top of the back of Jack Sparrow's chair make a classic Mickey.

Hint 46: On the right side as you exit, and before you reach the street outside, a classic Mickey-shaped lock adorns a back door to the Pieces of Eight shop.

New Orleans Square

Hint 47: Walt and Roy Disney's gold stylized initials are in the blue railing above the Royal Street Veranda.

- *Haunted Mansion*

Hint 48: As soon as you walk through the front door along the entrance queue, go to any of the candlestick holders on the wall and, with your back to the wall, look up from underneath to spot a classic Mickey effect.

Hint 49: Large circles form classic Mickeys in the wallpaper of the Art Gallery after you exit the Stretching Room.

Hint 50: As you pass by the "endless hallway" in your Doom Buggy, check out the back of the purple chair for an abstract Donald Duck. Near the top of the chair, you can see his cap, which sits above his distorted eyes, face and bill. (Note: The chair location may change at times.)

Hint 51: In the Séance room, a floating table above you has a tilted classic Mickey design at the top of the legs and just below the tabletop.

Hint 52: In the Ballroom scene, "snow" may dust the floor at the right rear of the room. When it does, a classic Mickey formed of snow is usually somewhere in the snowdrift.

Hint 53: During the Ballroom scene, look down at the place settings near the center of the dining table. You'll see two small saucers and one larger plate forming a classic Mickey. The Cast Members move this Hidden Mickey around at times.

Hint 54: After the ballroom scene, look to the right as soon as you enter the attic. Find the clock on a bureau to the right of the oval portrait of a bride and groom and just to the right of a bright orange and blue lamp. A brown classic Mickey hides behind the pendulum of the clock.

Frontierland
- *The Golden Horseshoe*

Hint 55: Walk toward the front of the stage and find a grate (or vent) in the center of the lower front wall. Start at the lower right hole in the grate. Then look up and diagonally left one hole to spot a classic Mickey hole in the grating.

Hint 56: Look for the "Hall of Fame" picture on the left wall lower level. Sideways gold classic Mickeys hide at the middle sides of the frame around Betty Taylor's picture.

Adventureland

- *Indiana Jones Adventure*

Hint 57: A full-body painting of Mara is on the wall to your right just as you enter the inside part of the queue. She is pouring coins, jewels, and pearls out of a bowl. An upside-down classic Mickey made of pearls is at the lower end of the long string of pearls.

57

Hint 58: Across from the first drinking fountains in the inside standby queue, Mickey's initials, "MM" in Mara script, are on the left wall, just above a horizontal crack in the wall.

Hint 59: On the side of a bamboo structure just opposite the hanging rope, a large painted stone slab has a tiny light blue classic Hidden Mickey symbol on the lower right edge of the circle of symbols around Mara's face. (Note: This image is becoming fainter with time and may disappear.)

Hint 60: On the ceiling, Mara's giant nose is a classic Mickey.

Hint 61: When you enter the room showing the video on a screen, study the left wall for a large classic Hidden Mickey between the last two lights on the wall.

Hint 62: *Indiana Jones Adventure* was built over a previous Eeyore (cast) parking lot. As a tribute to the past, an original white parking sign in the shape of Eeyore was placed in the video room, high up in the rafters. To spot it, go to the end of the video room, turn around, and look up to the left of the projector. If you can't find it, ask a nearby Cast Member for help.

Hint 63: In an office just past the video room, Mickey and Minnie Mouse are pictured on a partially visible magazine cover. The magazine is on a desktop. (Note: These magazine images are moved around and may not be visible at times.)

Hint 64: Shortly after the ride starts, look at Mara's face for a (not quite perfect) classic Mickey formed by the curves of the nostrils and the oval depression just below the middle of the nose.

Hint 65: As soon as your vehicle turns a corner and enters the Mummy Room, look left for a skeleton wearing a Mickey Mouse hat. Let's hope the hat stays put!

New Orleans Square

- Disneyland Railroad

Hint 66: Spot the agriculture ("Agrifuture") sign from the train just past "it's a small world" after leaving Mickey's Toontown station. Above the peach stem in the sign, the top three grapes in the bunch of grapes come together to form a classic Mickey.

Frontierland

-Mark Twain Riverboat/ Sailing Ship Columbia

Hint 67: As you cruise along, watch for a bridge on the left side of the river, and find the second vertical side post (of the wire mesh fence) from the left end of the bridge span. A small classic Hidden Mickey washer is under the second bolt from the top of this post.

Hint 68: Continue to study the bridge. In the shadows under the right side of the bridge is a large black classic Mickey hole in the rock.

Hint 69: Study the metal grillwork between the smokestacks and high above the *Mark Twain's* prow for a sideways classic Mickey.

Hint 70: To the right of the entrance for the *Mark Twain Riverboat* is a "Shipping Office." A painting advertising river excursions on the *Mark Twain* hangs on an "office" wall. In the painting, Mickey Mouse is one of the passengers on the lowest deck.

- Tom Sawyer Island

Hint 71: As you exit the Raft onto the island, turn left and look above the first cavern entrance you encounter. A classic Mickey depression is in the rock over the middle of the entrance opening.

Hint 72: Stroll into *Dead Man's Grotto* cave. Near the end of the cavern walkway inside, a jail cell is secured with two Mickey-shaped locks at the ends of a long chain.

Hint 73: Stroll back to the heaps of coins in the *Pirate 's Lair* play area. At the right rear of the coin heaps, look in front of the hanging blue pirate tarp for a wood plank that holds the treasure in place. Three coins on the ground that peek out from under the right side of the wood plank form a classic Hidden Mickey.

Critter Country

- Splash Mountain

Hint 74: A tiny classic Mickey is formed of indentations in a protruding knot on a post at the beginning of the outside stand-by entrance queue. Mickey is on the post just below the *Splash Mountain* Warning sign. You can also spot this Mickey as you exit *Haunted Mansion*.

Hint 75: As you enter the inside part of the entrance queue, look along the left side for a three-gear classic Mickey.

Hint 76: At the top of the last big climb, just before the big drop, three rocks stuck in the ceiling form a distorted sideways classic Mickey, facing left.

Tomorrowland

- Near Finding Nemo Submarine Voyage & the Monorail exit

Hint 77: From the *Disneyland Monorail* loading area or exit in Tomorrowland, you can often spot a classic Mickey made of coiled rope lying near the end of the Finding Nemo Submarine Voyage dock.

Hint 78: A classic Mickey impression is in the rock wall about one foot off the floor and between two separated hand-rails.

- Finding Nemo: Marine Observation Outpost

Hint 79: Look for the lockers on the left front wall inside the *Marine Observation Outpost*. You can spot Sorcerer Mickey inside locker No. 105. He's on the clothing that's under a pair of sunglasses.

-Autopia

Hint 80: A black classic Mickey hides in the upper right corner of the car license plates.

Afternoon Parade

- Grand Marshal automobile

Hint 81: On this attractive replica of an antique touring car, classic Mickeys adorn the tires, the front bumper, the hood ornament, nuts at the side of the front windshield, the tread on the spare tire on the rear of the car, and the brackets holding the spare tire in place.

Fantasyland

- *Mickey and the Magical Map Show*

Hint 82: On the right upper corner of the decorative archway above the stage, three yellow circles form an up-side-down classic Hidden Mickey.

Hint 83: A gold classic Mickey made of circles hides in the middle of a stained-glass window at the far left side of the stage set. This Hidden Mickey is best viewed from close to the stage.

Hint 84: At various times during the show, you can see classic Mickey circles near the top of the stained-glass design at the right rear of the stage. The classic Mickey is tilted slightly to the left.

Hint 85: When the stage map opens up during the "Under the Sea" segment of the show, some blue classic Hidden Mickey bubbles are inside larger bubbles on the rear screen.

Hint 86: During the "Under the Sea" segment of the show, a three-bubble classic Mickey floats up the left side of the rear screen.

Hint 87: During the show, Mickey interacts with an elusive black splotch. At one point, just for a second, the round splotch morphs into a classic Mickey! Watch for it just after the "Under the Sea" segment.

- *Fantasy Faire*

Hint 88: Locate Clopin's Music Box for some interesting images. (To refresh, Clopin is the leader of the gypsies in the Disney movie *The Hunchback of Notre Dame*.) Look to the far left inside the Music Box to spot a tiny classic Mickey at the top of the second window from the left.

Hint 89: Many Disney characters are mixed in the crowd of people inside Clopin's Music Box, including Flynn Rider, Snow White, Doc, Sleepy, Peter Pan, Mr. Smee, Maurice, Belle, the Beast in human form, Gaston, a man from Gaston's tavern, Tony (from Lady and the Tramp), Geppetto, and the evil coachman who takes Pinocchio to Pleasure Island.

Frontierland

- *Big Thunder Mountain Railroad*

Hint 90: An upside-down classic Hidden Mickey is formed of round rust or stain circles that surround bullet holes on the back of a wooden "Standby Entrance" sign in front of the attraction. The Mickey circles are next to an Ace of Clubs nailed to the back of the sign.

Hint 91: As you start to climb the second hill, look to your left, near the bottom of the hill, for three gears that form a large, upside-down classic Mickey.

Hint 92: On your right as you exit, three of the highest green lobes in the cactus garden usually form an oval classic Mickey. At times, other collections of cactus lobes may also form Mickeys.

Adventureland

- *Jungle Cruise*

Hint 93: Beneath the outside *Jungle Cruise* sign, a mask that resembles Donald Duck hangs just above the entrance.

Hint 94: Along the entrance queue, inside a caged display entitled "Safari Staging Area," a bag with a camera and other provisions lies against the side of the display next to the part of the queue near the loading area. Three lenses on the camera form a classic Hidden Mickey.

Hint 95: At the left front of the gorilla camp scene to the right of the boat, three pieces of dinnerware – a plate for the "head" and two round shallow bowls for the "ears" – come together as a classic Mickey tilted to the left.

Hint 96: Listen for chanting and dancing natives on the right side of your boat; some are blowing long curved horns. Behind and to the right of the horn blowers, an image of Mufasa from *The Lion King* decorates a brown shield that stands in front of a straw hut.

Hint 97: Along the left side of the boat, be alert for menacing natives with spears. The next to last isolated native of the group wears a Donald mask.

- *Tarzan's Treehouse*

Hint 98: Behind the ship's wheel, the far right curtain knobs at the right rear of the room form a classic Mickey. The curtain knobs directly to the left resemble a classic Mickey as well.

Hint 99: Pots that resemble Mrs. Potts and Chip from the *Beauty and the Beast* movie sit alongside the trail in the children's play area near the end.

- Walt Disney's Enchanted Tiki Room

Hint 100: Four shields hang over the *Enchanted Tiki Room* exit. A classic Mickey with two smiley faces for "ears" hides near the bottom of the left shield.

Mickey's Toontown

- Near the entrance

Hint 101: A white silhouette of Mickey's face and ears, seen from the front, adorns the "Order of Mouse" seal on the overhead bridge to the left of the "Welcome to Mickey's Toontown" sign.

- In and outside of Minnie's House

Hint 102: Inside the refrigerator in Minnie's kitchen, a bottle of cheese relish on the second shelf in the door has a red classic Mickey "brand mark" at the top of the label.

Hint 103: To the right of the large blue doors that lead backstage near *Minnie's House*, a small opening leads to a "Cast Members Only" entrance and exit. Walk into this opening and look left to spot a blue rock classic Mickey in the wall.

Hint 104: Above and behind the left side of the large blue doors that lead backstage near Minnie's House, you can see the top of the large letters "W" and "D" for "Walt Disney." The "W" is dark green, and the "D" is a lighter green.

- *Approaching, in, and exiting Mickey's House*

Hint 105: The window in Mickey's green front door is a partial classic-Mickey shape.

Hint 106: The welcome mat at Mickey's front door is shaped like a classic Mickey.

Hint 107: As you enter the first room, stop by the green, glass-fronted bookcase. The top of the spine of the book "2001: A Mouse Odyssey" is decorated with two gold classic Mickeys.

Hint 108: In the same bookcase, find the orange book, "See You Next Squeak." At the bottom of the spine, the publisher's logo is a classic Mickey enclosed in a square.

Hint 109: At the left side of the first room, the bottom of the spine of the blue book entitled "My Fair Mouse" sports a side-profile Mickey.

Hint 110: Just as you enter the piano room, study the bookcase on the right side. On the right upper shelf, the book "My Life with Walt" has a pink classic Mickey at the top of the spine.

Hint 111: In the same bookcase, locate the book "Pluto's Republic." To its immediate left, a thin green book has a yellow classic Mickey at the top of its spine.

Hint 112: Most of the holes in the paper for the player piano are classic Mickeys, but one of the holes is shaped like Goofy! You can spot him at times through the left side glass, next to the center green wood post.

Hint 113: The weight for the metronome on top of the player piano is a classic Mickey.

Hint 114: In the room with Mickey's drums, look for a drum with legs on the lower shelf. Knobs along its rim sport Mickey ears.

Hint 115: Also in the room with Mickey's drums, Mickey's gloves are on the hour and minute hands of a cuckoo clock on the wall.

Hint 116: There is a mirror on the right side inside *Mickey's Movie Barn*. Stare at it and wait awhile. Mickey Mouse's head will appear.

Hint 117: On your left as you continue walking, a paintbrush on the top right of Donald Duck's wooden workbench has pink paint splotches that form an upside-down classic Mickey.

Hint 118: Also in *Mickey's Movie Barn* (and before you meet Mickey Mouse in person), a classic Mickey appears around the countdown numbers on the screen before the film starts.

Hint 119: Mickey's red car sits outside his house in his driveway. The car's hubcaps and spare tire sport white classic Mickeys.

Hint 120: Outside the exit from *Mickey's House*, classic Mickeys hide in the decorative ironwork on a lamp sitting on a short post.

- *Clarabelle's Snack Stand*
Hint 121: A shutter is pulled down when *Clarabelle's Snack Stand* closes for business. A white classic Mickey marking is on the left side of the shutter.

67

- *Toontown Post Office*

Hint 122: At the Post Office, Mickey is on the postage stamp on the letter above the entrance. You'll also find a side profile of Mickey (along with five other decorative characters) inside the Post Office on the wall mounted mailboxes.

- *Toontown Fire Department*

Hint 123: When you ring the doorbell at the Fire Department, move back quickly to spot the Dalmatian puppy who looks out of an upper middle window for a few seconds. A sideways classic Mickey made of black spots is on his upper forehead.

- *Fireworks Factory*

Hint 124: Face the *Fireworks Factory* and find a small, pink firework cone poking out from the right wall. It's one of the lower fireworks, and it has a small, blue classic Mickey painted halfway up its cone.

- *Goofy's Playhouse*

Hint 125: A child with a classic Mickey head stands with an adult at the bottom of the *Goofy's Playhouse* signpost in front of the outside play area.

Critter Country

- *The Many Adventures of Winnie the Pooh*

Hint 126: The back and lower legs of the "Heffabee" on top of each ride vehicle form an upside-down classic Mickey.

Hint 127: In the first part of the entrance

tunnel, a small classic Hidden Mickey hides on the bark of a round tree trunk that you reach just before you get to the wall covered with colorful leaves. Mickey's to the right of your vehicle, at about eye level.

Hint 128: As you leave the Heffalump and Woozle room, turn around in your vehicle and look up behind you to see Max the buck, Buff the buffalo, and Melvin the moose hanging on the wall above you. (These three animals pay homage to the original attractions in this location-the *Country Bear Jamboree* and then the *Country Bear Playhouse*.)

Hint 129: After the Heffalump and Woozle room, there is a Heffalump collage on your right. Look in the bottom right-hand corner to spot an upsidedown classic Mickey.

- *Pooh Corner store*

Hint 130: In the room with candies and treats, find a window where you can watch Cast Members prepare treats. On the wall inside and opposite the window are pictures referencing the *Country Bear Jamboree*, which was replaced by *The Many Adventures of Winnie the Pooh*. One picture shows Winnie the Pooh sitting on Gomer the Bear's piano and in another picture, Pooh extends a hand to Teddi Barra.

- *Briar Patch store*

Hint 131: Three yarn balls (white "head" with a white "ear" and a black "ear") come together as a classic Mickey in the middle of a jar sitting on a high shelf at the left rear of the store.

Fantasyland

- Alice in Wonderland

Hint 132: As you go down the rabbit hole, watch in front of you for a small house (the White Rabbit's house). A tiny, almost upside-down classic Mickey sits at the upper left corner of a frame (of a picture or mirror) on a wall that you can see through the front window of the upper level of the house. Look in the center of the open window for the Hidden Mickey.

Hint 133: When the cards are "painting the roses red," look on the ground under the tree to the left for a slightly distorted red classic Mickey. It's on a third-level ledge under the right hand with the paintbrush and just to the left of a green heart.

- Storybook Land Canal Boats

Hint 134: On the middle of one side of the vertical strut at the rear of the "Daisy" boat, an upside-down classic Mickey is made of round flowers-a yellow "head" and pink "ears."

Hint 135: On the rear side of the "Flora" boat, a small purple classic Mickey is hiding in the flower design.

Hint 136: A classic Mickey formed of purple berries hangs on a vine on the back of the pilot's seat on the "Snow White" boat. One of the bluebirds in the painting is eyeing those special berries.

Hint 137: On the "Wendy" boat, a classic Mickey in relief hides on the upper back of the rear post.

Hint 138: On the boat ride, after passing through Monstro the Whale, watch for Pinocchio's Village on your right. As you float in front of the first house in the village, look past the first two blue-roofed houses to the rear row of buildings which are visible only for a few seconds. A tiny classic Hidden Mickey is at the upper left of a yellow shield, which is on the left side of the front wall of a building with a gray roof.

Hint 139: The pumpkin carriage on the upper road approaching Cinderella's village simulates an upside-down classic Mickey. The pumpkin is the "head" and the side wheels are the "ears."

- *Pinocchio's Daring Journey*

Hint 140: As you approach the ride vehicles in the entrance queue, scan the scene across the ride track for a small flower pot in front of a blue door. Three flowers at the lower right of the group of flowers come together as a classic Hidden Mickey, sideways to the left.

Hint 141: When your vehicle enters the Pleasure Island room, study the ground in front of the popcorn stand on your right. Some "spilled" popcorn forms a classic Hidden Mickey.

Hint 142: Look back at the left side window in the popcorn stand for an upside-down classic Mickey in the popcorn, about one-third the way up in the window.

Hint 143: Near the end of the ride, in Geppetto's workshop, a fish is near the top of a glass globe which sits on a wooden stand covered with ornate carvings. An upright three-circle Hidden

Mickey is carved into the right side of the flat upper portion of the stand.

Hint 144: Near the end of the ride a big case holds a model ship. The middle of the top frame of the case is decorated with a wooden classic Mickey.

- *Snow White's Scary Adventures*

Hint 145: A somewhat distorted three-quarter side-profile Mickey is formed by bushes in the mural directly in front of your ride vehicle at the loading area. Look at the right end of the row of green bushes just past the rocky hill and to the left of the blue stream. Mickey is looking to the rig ht. His nose is in front of the bush at the right side that hangs over the stream.

Hint 146: Early on in the ride, look for the green turtle climbing the stairs to the left of your ride vehicle. The large circle on the left side of the turtle's shell forms the "head" of a three-circle classic Mickey on the shell.

Hint 147: As you pass through the dwarfs' mine, stay alert for the mine car full of bright jewels on your left. A green Tinker Bell is on the back wall behind and to the upper left of the mine car.

- *"it's a small world"*

Hint 148: Three circular control towers topped by umbrellas overlook the entrance queue. The center tower is larger than the other two, so together they form a classic Mickey.

Hint 149: Disney characters appear alongside your tour boa t. Look for Alice in Wonderland, Cinderella, Pinocchio, Ariel, Nemo and Dory, Lilo and Stitch, Jessie and Woody, and others.

Hint 150: Early in your boat ride, look above you for a boy standing in a hot air balloon with a toy bear holding on to the ropes to the boy's right. The bear's head and ears cast a classic Hidden Mickey shadow on the balloon.

Hint 151: Watch for koala bears hanging on a tree. The head and ears of several of the bears simulate Mickey's head.

Hint 152: In the last room of the ride, shadows from groups of small balloons that move up and down form classic Mickeys on the ceiling at times above your boat.

- King Arthur Carrousel

Hint 153: Find the white horse, Jingles. Classic Mickeys made of gemstones are on the front and back of the horse. These classic Mickeys aren't perfectly proportioned, and the "ears" and "head" don't touch, but they seem purposeful. (Jingles is also adorned with images from the *Mary Poppins* movie.)

- The Mad Hatter

Hint 154: Every few minutes, a faint image of the Cheshire Cat appears in the mirror above the store's check-out area.

Hint 155: A Mickey hat with ears hides at one corner of each of two outdoor signs for the shop.

- Castle Heraldry Shoppe

Hint 156: Near the *Castle Heraldry Shoppe*, a classic Mickey is in the bottom center of the painted scroll trim at the edges of an outdoor mailbox. Also look for the classic Mickeys wearing "Mickey's Sorcerer's Hat." They're repeated at the end of some of the branches in the scrollwork at the top and bottom.

Tomorrowland

- The Star Trader

Hint 157: Classic Mickey holes are in some of the shop's upright merchandise display poles.

Hint 158: Some merchandise bins have classic Mickey feet and classic Mickey holes encircling the top rim.

- Little Green Men Store Command

Hint 159: A green side profile of Mickey Mouse hides on a planet at the middle right edge of the sign for this store near *Buzz Lightyear Astro Blasters*.

- Astro Orbitor

Hint 160: The moving spheres above the *Astro Orbitor* occasionally form classic Mickeys.

Frontierland

- Entrance walkway from the central hub

Hint 161: A cannon sits to the right, just past the Frontierland sign on the entrance walkway from the central hub. In the tongue behind the cannon is a classic Mickey, formed by a hole and two bolts.

- Frontierland Shootin' Exposition

Hint 162: In front of the "Nancy's Dan" tombstone, three lobes of a cactus resemble a classic Mickey.

- Pioneer Mercantile shop

Hint 163: On the walls inside the gift shop, white river rocks at the lower center of some of the lamp covers (the ones with bears) form classic Mickeys.

- Rancho del Zocalo Restaurante

Hint 164: Halfway up a wooden support post near the corner of a wall behind a condiment and napkin cart, you can spot a classic Mickey depression in the wood. You'll see it best by looking back in from the exit with the gate on the restaurant's right side (as you approach the restaurant from the main Frontierland walkway).

Main Street, U.S.A.

- Plaza Inn restaurant

Hint 165: To the right of the main entrance (as you enter), a framed painting of a floral arrangement includes an upside-down classic Mickey formed of roses.

- Photo Supply Company

Hint 166: On the middle of a high shelf behind the "Photo Preview" counter, a lens and two adjoining circles form a classic Mickey on the front of a small camera.

- Silhouette Studio

Hint 167: In the front display window of the *Silhouette Studio*, the fancy frames on some of the displays include classic Mickeys. (These frames come and go, but a frame with classic Mickeys is almost always on display.)

- Fruit cart

Hint 168: A classic Mickey hides on an axle under a fruit cart that is usually positioned midway along Main Street near the Disney Clothiers shop.

- In and near Main Street Cinema

Hint 169: Inside *Main Street Cinema*, some of the recessed lights on the front of the step risers are shaped like classic Mickeys.

Hint 170: Outside, near *Main Street Cinema*, a "Casting Agency" sign on a door includes two classic Mickeys in the design, one at the top and one at the bottom.

- Main Street Magic Shop

Hint 171: Along the front counter inside the *Magic Shop*, a white rope on a display shelf is coiled into a classic Mickey shape.

Hint 172: In an outside display window to the left of the *Magic Shop's* entrance, the ace on an Ace of Clubs playing card resembles a classic Mickey instead of a club.

- *Penny Arcade*

Hint 173: Along the rear wall, a small classic Mickey hides between the play buttons on a game machine called "Pinocchio, Make Him Dance."

- *Gibson Girl Ice Cream Parlor*

Hint 174: The words "Ice Cream Floats" are on an outside window to the right. A tiny classic Mickey is midway up the right leg of the letter "A" in the word "Floats."

- *Emporium store*

Hint 175: Walk into the store through the entrance facing Main Street. (It's at the end of the store closest to City Hall.) Look behind the cashier's counter to your right as you enter the store and search the wall for a still-life painting with flowers. A distorted but recognizable image of Sorcerer Mickey is on a blue globe, which sits on a small table in the painting.

Hint 176: Check out a room with toys at the end of the store closest to Carnation Cafe. A toy train makes a circuit on a track above you along the walls. Stand near the small water tower at one corner of the room. Every third or so trip around the track, the train stops in front of the water tower, and a classic Hidden Mickey lights up at the upper right side of the tower. You can also usually spot the faint Hidden Mickey image when it's not lit up.

- *above The Mad Hatter*

Hint 177: To the left of the Opera House, Disney sculptor Blaine Gibson is honored in one of the middle second-floor windows above *The Mad Hatter*. At the upper part of the window, under the words "The Busy Hands," two hands hold a blue carving. A classic Hidden Mickey forms the right end of the carving.

- Disneyland Railroad: Main Street Station

Hint 178: Classic Mickey-shaped holes are drilled into metal brackets behind the conductor's cabin on top of several of the tender tanks, for example, "Fred Gurley's" Engine No. 3 and "Ward Kimball's" Engine No. 5. You can spot these classic Mickeys from the side waiting queue or from inside the first car.

Frontierland

- Fantasmic!

Hint 179: During the *Fantasmic!* show, a classic Mickey appears on the water screen, outlined by white foam. You can spot it at the lower part of the water screen, after Monstro the Whale appears and just before the scene with Mickey and the whirlpool.

Hint 180: A magic mirror is projected on the water screen at one point in the show, and you'll see the faces of various villains in the mirror. Three circles at the bottom of the gold mirror frame come together as a classic Mickey.

Fireworks show

Hint 181: Disneyland's fireworks show often features a cluster of three exploding shells that form a classic Mickey.

Entrance Plaza between the theme parks

Hint 182: Some of the engraved personalized brick plaques at your feet along the entrance plaza feature a bell design. The bell ringer is a classic Mickey. (You'll also find decorative Mickey images on these plaques.)

Hint 183: Take a look at the directional signpoles. You'll find classic Mickey indentations on the bottoms of some of them, while the tops of the poles sport Mickey ears.

Notes

Disney California Adventure Scavenger Hunt

*
Arrive at the entrance turnstiles (with your admission ticket) 45 minutes before the opening time for early entry (if you're eligible) or 45 minutes before the official opening time if you're not or if it's a nonearly entry day.

*
Hotfoot it to Cars Land. Line up for **_Radiator Springs Racers_**.

Clue 1: Take note of some cactuses along the standby entrance queue.
3 points

Clue 2: Look for a Hidden Mickey inside the Stanley's Cap 'n' Tap area of the standby entrance queue.
3 points

Clue 3: On the ride, if you go through Ramone's Body Art shop, keep your eyes peeled for Mickey on a wall -mounted electrical box.
5 points

Clue 4: On the ride, if you go through Luigi's tire shop, watch behind Luigi for Hidden Mickeys.
5 points

Clue 5: If you go through Luigi's tire shop, spot Mickey on a red tool box.
5 points

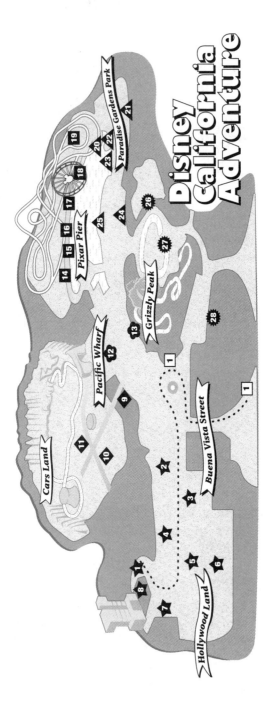

Disney California Adventure®

Buena Vista Street
1. Red Car Trolley (Reopens in 2020)

Hollywood Land
2. Disney Junior Dance Party
3. Mickey's PhilharMagic
4. Disney Animation:
   - Sorcerer's Workshop
   - Anna & Elsa's Royal Welcome
   - Animation Academy
   - Turtle Talk with Crush
5. The Hollywood Backlot Stage
6. Monsters, Inc. Mike & Sulley to the Rescue!
7. Frozen – Live at the Hyperion
8. Guardians of the Galaxy – Mission: BREAKOUT!
9. Splash Mountain

Cars Land
10. Luigi's Rollickin' Roadsters
11. Radiator Springs Racers

Pacific Wharf
12. The Bakery Tour
13. Walt Disney Imagineering Blue Sky Cellar

Pixar Pier
14. Incredicoaster
15. Jessie's Critter Carousel
16. Toy Story Midway Mania!
17. Games of Pixar Pier
18. Pixar Pal-A-Round
19. Inside Out Emotional Whirlwind

Paradise Gardens Park
20. Silly Symphony Swings
21. Goofy's Sky School
22. Jumpin' Jellyfish
23. Golden Zephyr
24. The Little Mermaid – Ariel's Undersea Adventure
25. World of Color

Grizzly Peak
26. Redwood Creek Challenge Trail
27. Grizzly River Run
28. Soarin' Around the World

83

*
Get a FASTPASS for *Guardians of the Galaxy - Mission: BREAKOUT!*

*
Your next mission is to get a FAST-PASS for the evening *World of Color* show. Recently, the distribution area for this FASTPASS was located across from the restrooms near the entrance to *The Little Mermaid -Ariel's Undersea Adventure.*

*
Pass by Lamplight Lounge and line up for ***Toy Story Midway Mania!***

Clue 6: Along the entrance queue, search for a tiny Hidden Mickey on a poster.
4 points

Clue 7: Spot a classic Mickey at the loading dock.
2 points

Clue 8: During the first part of the ride, stay alert for the title of a board game from Walt Disney.
5 points

Clue 9: On an interactive screen as you ride, look behind the target balloons in front of the volcano for a classic Mickey.
5 points

Clue 10: On another screen, watch the white plates for a classic Mickey image.
4 points

Clue 11: Find Mickey after you exit your vehicle.
4 points

*
Walk past *Pixar Pal-A-Round* to ***Goofy's Sky School.***

Clue 12: As you approach *Goofy's Sky School*, admire a sign for a Hidden Mickey.
2 points

Clue 13: In the standby entrance queue, study two bulletin boards for two subtle Hidden Mickeys.
10 points for finding both

Clue 14: As you exit the ride vehicle, locate Mickey on a tool.
3 points

*
Go to **Monsters, Inc. Mike & Sulley to the Rescue!** and line up.

Clue 15: Study the inside queue walls for a Hidden Mickey.
3 points

Clue 16: Watch the pre-show video monitor in the queue for a Hidden Mickey.
3 points

Clue 17: Before you board your vehicle, spot those headlights again!
2 points

Clue 18: At the beginning of the ride, search the skyline for a tiny Hidden Mickey.
5 points

Clue 19: Don't miss the moving Mickey shadow on a wall along the ride! Concentrate on the left wall.
5 points

Clue 20: Admire the color-changing Randall (the multi-legged lizard-shaped monster) for a Hidden Mickey!
5 points

Clue 21: On the ride, look for a Hidden Mickey on Sulley.
4 points

Clue 22: Stay alert for Mickey near a monitor screen.
3 points

*
Ride **Guardians of the Galaxy - Mission: BREAKOUT!** at your FAST-PASS time.

Clue 23: Look up for a Hidden Figment in the first room of the entrance queue.
5 points

Clue 24: If you proceed to the right, study display items in the second room for a Mickey face.
5 bonus points

Clue 25: If you approach the far right ride lift on the lower level, look around for a Mickey lock.
3 points

*
Get a FASTPASS for *Soarin' Around the World* (or *Soarin' Over California*). Over in Cars Land, check out the entrance queue for **Luigi 's Rollickin' Roadsters**.

Clue 26: Look for a tiny Lightning McQueen with Mickey ears.
4 points

Clue 27: Find a drawing of a small red car with a Mickey-shaped headlight.
4 points

Clue 28: Search nearby for an upside-down classic Mickey.
3 points

*
Enter the queue for **Mater's Junkyard Jamboree**.

Clue 29: Search above you for a classic Mickey.
4 points

Clue 30: While in the queue, glance around the ride surface area for a Hidden Mickey, then enjoy the attraction if you wish. Or exit without riding to search for the next Hidden Mickey.
3 points

*
During your FASTPASS window, enjoy **Soarin' Around the World** (or **Soarin' Over California** - see below).

Clue 31: Pay attention to the pre-show video for Mickey ears.
2 points

Clue 32: Also in the pre-show video, find some clothing characters.
4 points for spotting two Hidden Characters

Clue 33: During the ride, search the hills to the left of the castle in Germany for a Hidden Mickey near a footbridge.
5 points

Clue 34: Focus on the desert sky for a floating Hidden Mickey.
5 points

Clue 35: Study the Fiji island for a small classic Mickey.
5 points

Clue 36: Look for some floating Mickeys below you near the end of the ride.
4 points

Clue 37: A huge classic Mickey in the sky greets you at the end of your ride.
3 points

[If **Soarin' Over California** is showing –

Clue 38: Pay attention to the pre-show video for Mickey ears.
2 points

Clue 39: Also in the pre-show video, find some clothing characters.
4 points for spotting two Hidden Characters

Clue 40: While on the ride, look left for a Mickey balloon when you see the golf course.
4 points

Clue 41: Now quickly look right for a Mickey shadow on the golf course.
4 points

Clue 42: Watch the golf ball hurtling toward you.
5 points

Clue 43: Look for some floating Mickeys below you near the end of the ride.
4 points

Clue 44: A huge classic Mickey in the sky greets you at the end of your ride.
5 points]

*
Get a FASTPASS for *Incredicoaster*.

*
Consider lunch at the restaurant of your choice or try one of the counter-service eateries such as Flo's V8 Cafe, Pacific Wharf Cafe, Cocina Cucamonga Mexican Grill, or Paradise Garden Grill.
 - While at lunch, check your Times Guide or Disneyland app for convenient show times for *Disney Junior Dance Party* and the *Five & Dime show* in Carthay Circle.

*
  At a convenient time, visit **Disney Junior Dance Party**.

Clue 45: Watch for small Mickey images on the main screen during the show.
5 points for spotting five or more

Clue 46: Find some Hidden Mickeys in a window of the *Disney Junior Dance Party* building.
3 points for 3 or more small Hidden Mickeys

*
  Amble over to Carthay Circle for the **Five & Dime show** you selected.

Clue 47: Study the car in the show.
3 points

*
  Enter Hollywood Land, then stand outside the **Disney Animation Building**.

Clue 48: Look up for a Hidden Mickey on a pole.
3 points

Clue 49: Now search for Mickey on the outside wall of the *Animation Building*.
2 points total for one or more

Clue 50: Search for a classic Hidden Mickey high above the stage inside the *Animation Academy*.
3 points

Clue 51: While inside *Animation Academy*, look for another classic Mickey on the Animator's desk.
2 points

Clue 52: Don't leave yet! Notice anything in the carpet?
3 points

*
Walk through the *Sorcerer's Workshop*.

Clue 53: Locate two Hidden Mickeys on
the wall.
4 points for spotting both

Clue 54: Stroll back to the *Beast's
Library* for a hot Hidden Mickey.
2 points

Clue 55: Spot Hidden Mickeys along the
Animation Building's exit hall.
3 points total for one or more

Clue 56: Find a Hidden Mickey in a wall
poster outside.
2 points

Clue 57: Search a display window
nearby for a Hidden Mickey.
3 points

Clue 58: Look for Mickey on the ceiling
inside the *Off the Page* store.
4 points

*
Cross the street to **Schmoozies**.

Clues 59, 60, and 61: Check out the
outside walls for Hidden Mickeys.
5 points total for finding three Hidden
Mickeys

Clue 62: Spot Minnie Mouse behind
the order windows!
5 points

*
At your FASTPASS time, walk to **Incredicoaster** and ride if you're brave
enough!

Clue 63: While you're screaming, stay
alert for a classic Mickey below you on
the ground.
4 points

*
Mosey to the **Redwood Creek Challenge Trail** in Grizzly Peak.

Clue 64: Tarry at the large trail map just inside the entrance and spot three classic Mickeys.
5 points for finding all three

Clue 65: Find a Mickey reference in the Mt. Whitney Lookout.
5 points

*
Check out the **Rushin' River Outfitters** shop near Grizzly River Run.

Clue 66: Search for Hidden Mickeys on the merchandise inside the shop.
3 points

*
Walk past the entrance to **Grizzly River Run** to the fence overlooking the raft stream.

Clue 67: Investigate the area near the fence for a Hidden Mickey.
4 points

*
Stroll to Paradise Gardens Park and enjoy **The Little Mermaid - Ariel's Undersea Adventure**.

Clue 68: Look for Mickey along the outside entrance queue.
2 points

Clue 69: Can you see Mickey in the lights?
2 points

Clue 70: In the entrance queue, search for a classic Mickey on top of a scallop shell.
3 points

Clue 71: Don't miss the Hidden Mickey on the loading dock mural!
4 points

Clue 72: Look near the feet of Scuttle – the talking seagull – for a Hidden Mickey.
4 Points

Clue 73: As you enter the room where the "Under the Sea" song is playing, study the purple coral for a classic Mickey.
4 points

Clue 74: Watch the spinning purple octopus for a Hidden Mickey.
4 points

Clue 75: Three Hidden Images are near the singing Ariel. Stare below her for the first one: a coral Hidden Mickey.
4 points

Clue 76: Locate a green fish nearby who is wearing a small, blue classic Mickey.
5 points

Clue 77: Now look quickly to your right across the track for a Hidden Mr. Limpet!
5 points

Clue 78: Check out the frogs along the ride!
4 points for one or more

Clue 79: Now look behind the frogs for a Hidden Mickey in the water.
4 points

Clue 80: Stay alert for a Hidden Surprise (two silhouettes) at the end of the ride, just before you exit your clam-mobile. It's a tribute to The Little Mermaid.
5 points

*
Approach *Walt Disney Imagineering Blue Sky Cellar*.

Clue 81: Say hello to Mickey at the entrance.
3 points

Clue 82: Explore inside *Blue Sky Cellar* for a container classic Mickey.
4 points

Clue 83: Enjoy other small Mickey images inside.
5 points for 5 or more

*
Wander behind *Blue Sky Cellar*.

Clue 84: Outside *Blue Sky Cellar*, look for Mickey in Pinot Grigio grapes.
4 points

*
Walk to Cars Land.

Clue 85: Gaze inside the office of the *Cozy Cone Motel* for a Hidden Cars movie character and a Hidden Mickey.
5 points for both

Clue 86: Mater poses at times for photos near the motel. Study him for a Hidden Mickey.
3 points

Clue 87: Outside the **Radiator Springs Curios Store**, check around for a classic Hidden Mickey.
5 points

Clue 88: Find a classic Mickey on the wall inside *Radiator Springs Curios Store*.
2 points

Clue 89: Glance up for Mickey inside the store.
2 points

*
Spend some time studying the six colorful car hoods in the outside display windows of **Ramone's House of Body Art**.

Clues 90 to 95: Mickey hides somewhere on each car hood! Start with the rightmost display window.
30 points for finding all six

Clue 96: Admire the purple car hood behind the front counter inside *Ramone's* and try to find Mickey.
5 points

Clue 97: Now spot Mickey on pillars inside the store.
2 points

Clue 98: Look around for Mickey images on merchandise boxes.
4 points for one or more

Clue 99: Outside *Ramone's House of Body Art*, search for Mickey near a pole.
4 points

*
Walkover to **The Bakery Tour** in nearby Pacific Wharf.

Clue 100: Look around for Mickey inside the entrance to the Tour.
2 points

*
Head to Pixar Pier and watch the action at **Jessie's Critter Carousel**.

Clue 101: Study an armadillo in the outer circle for a Hidden Mickey.
4 point

*
Step over to the **Jack-Jack Cookie Num Num**s stand.

Clue 102: Do you see a Hidden Mickey on a cookie?
3 points

* Stroll past *Incredicoaster* along the promenade.

Clue 103: Search for an upside-down Hidden Mickey on a billboard.
3 points

* Go to Paradise Gardens Park and stop by the **Seaside Souvenirs shop** near *Jumpin' Jellyfish*.

Clue 104: Find Mickey on a wall inside the shop.
3 points

Clue 105: Now spot two references to Jules Verne in this shop!
4 points for both

* It's time for more Hollywood Land magic! Mosey into **Mickey's PhilharMagic**.

Clue 106: In the show, look for a shadow Mickey on a table.
4 points

Clue 107: Stare at Ariel's jewels for a classic Mickey in a ring.
5 points

Clue 108: Keep alert for a classic Mickey during the magic carpet ride.
5 points

* Return to Buena Vista Street to find more Hidden Mickeys.

Clue 109: Look down along the entrance area in front of **Carthay Circle Restaurant** for a Hidden Mickey.
5 points

Clue 110: Inside **Clarabelle's Hand-Scooped Ice Cream Shop**, search for Mickey on a display bottle.
5 points

Clue 111: Find a Hidden Mickey in a window of the **Julius Katz & Sons** store.
2 points

Clue 112: Inside *Julius Katz & Sons*, search a top shelf for a Hidden Mickey.
4 points

Clue 113: Inside **Big Top Toys** store, locate a Hidden Mickey on a mural.
4 points

Clue 114: Near **Oswald's**, scan a blue advertisement on an outside wall for Mickey.
5 points

Clue 115: Spot a classic Mickey at the **Red Car Trolley Station** near the main park entrance.
3 points

*
  Exit Disney California Adventure Park to the **main entrance plaza**.

Clue 116: Look over the trees in the entrance plaza for Hidden Mickeys.
3 points

Clue 117: Check out some ticket buildings for Hidden Mickeys.
2 points

*
  Rest, relax, have some dinner, and plan on returning for the **World of Color** show in Paradise Bay.

Clue 118: Watch *World of Color* to spot a Mickey balloon. (Try to stand at the front of an elevated area).
5 points

96

Now total your score.

Total Points for Disney California Adventure Park =

How'd You Do?

Up to 165 points - Bronze
166 to 330 points - Silver
331 points and over - Gold
413 points - Perfect Score

You may have done even better if you earned bonus points in Monsters, Inc. Mike & Sulley to the Rescue! or in Guardians of the Galaxy – Mission: BREAKOUT!

Notes

If you need help, the Hints are here for you!

Cars Land

- *Radiator Springs Racers*

Hint 1: A classic Mickey made of three barrel cactuses sits on the ground along the right side of the standby entrance queue. It's just past a pole with a sign that says "Long Trip? One Sip and Watch Those Miles Melt Away."

Hint 2: Inside the Stanley's Cap 'n' Tap covered area along the standby entrance queue, a wedding photo of

Stanley and Lizzie is on a wall. A classic Mickey is formed of circles above Lizzie's forehead in the middle of her veil.

Hint 3: On the ride, if you go through Ramone's Body Art shop, look back to your right in the second room of the shop to spot a classic Mickey made of circles on an electrical box. It's on the right rear wall just past the doors between the rooms of Ramone's shop.

Hint 4: On the ride, if you go through Luigi's tire shop, glance in the window behind Luigi to spot moving light images that include small classic Mickey shapes.

Hint 5: Also in Luigi's tire shop, watch on your right for a red toolbox that sits behind a rack of tires. Three inner circles in a design on the side of the box form a classic Mickey.

Pixar Pier

- *Toy Story Midway Mania!*

Hint 6: Along the inside part of the winding entrance queue, spots near a blue dinosaur's left eye and upper horn form a classic Mickey, tilted to the right. The dino, Trixie from *Toy Story*, is near the right lower corner of a poster labeled "Dino Darts."

Hint 7: On the wall at the loading area, a classic Mickey is formed by three picture frames with *Toy Story* characters.

Hint 8: At the beginning of the ride, right after the practice round and as your vehicle scoots to the next stop, look back at the wall behind you for "Walt Disney's Adventureland game," which sits flat below the "Twister" game.

Hint 9: Watch for the screen with target balloons in front of the volcano spewing lava. If you pop the middle 100-point balloon on the second tier, a faint classic Mickey appears on the rear surface in the lava behind the balloons.

Hint 10: Be alert for the screen with moving white plates. At one point, a large front plate aligns with smaller plates behind it to form a classic Mickey.

Hint 11: Along the exit walkway from the ride, a "Toy Story Midway" game sits on a rug in a display room to the left. On the left side of the game box, three ovals (containing pictures of Jessie, Rex, and Bullseye the horse) form a classic Mickey.

Paradise Gardens Park

- *Goofy's Sky School*

Hint 12: As you walk toward *Goofy's Sky School*, look up at a sign for the attraction that shows Goofy flying a red plane. Three large holes in the sign form a sideways classic Mickey.

Hint 13: Along the standby entrance queue, check the walls for cork bulletin boards. On the first board, three round impressions in the cork form a classic Mickey. It's tilted to the right, and it's at the right lower side of the upside-down note that says, "Notice to Appear." A similar classic Hidden Mickey made of impressions is on a second bulletin board on another wall along the queue. This one is tilted to the left and is partially covered by the left side of a handwritten letter that says "Dear Teach." Look above the right upper corner of a note that reads "I Fix Planes!" to spot it.

Hint 14: As you exit the ride vehicle, look for a classic Mickey at the top of the handle of a wrench that's hanging on a wall at the far right of a tool rack.

Hollywood Land

- *Monsters, Inc. Mike & Sulley to the Rescue!*

Hint 15: On the "Monstropolis Cab Co." wall poster, the taxicab headlights form an upside-down classic Mickey.

Hint 16: During the video loop on the queue monitors, a taxi appears with the words "Please Proceed" on the front bum pe r. The headlights of this vehicle are shaped like upside-down classic Mickeys.

Hint 17: The taxi with the upside-down headlight classic Mickeys is pictured on the side of your vehicle.

Hint 18: As your vehicle begins to move, look at the skyline behind a tall wall to your left. A tiny black classic Mickey is visible through holes along the top of the wall. Look along the skyline. You'll find this Mickey below the green "Downtown" sign and to the left of a tall vertical pipe behind the wall.

Hint 19: To the left of your ride vehicle, a side-profile shadow of the main mouse moves from left to right - also a smaller side profile shadow of Mickey moves from right to left - along the windows in the wall of the Harryhausen's restaurant scene. (Try to spot his moving shadow on the right wall, too!)

Hint 20: Watch for "Boo" on top of Randall's back. She pounds on Randall's head with a bat, causing his camouflage coloration to change continually. At one point, his body turns lime green (or sometimes yellow) with a blue (or purple) classic Mickey spot on his belly above a lower leg. (Note: This great image is visible only intermittently and not on every ride-through. Good luck!)

Hint 21: Sulley appears several times during the ride. A dark classic Mickey marking is on Sulley's left upper thigh the last time he appears (by the pink door with the blue flower on it).

Hint 22: Near the end of the ride, a classic Mickey is formed by dials and gauges on a control panel under the right monitor screen.

- Guardians of the Galaxy- Mission: BREAKOUT!

Hint 23: Inside the first room along the entrance queue, various creatures are imprisoned in electrified glass cases suspended from the ceiling. You can barely make out Figment's head and arms as he stands in a case (usually with light brown lighting) in the middle of the left side (as you face the video screen across the room) of the group of cases above you.

Hint 24: On the right side, in the second room (the Collector's office), along the wall to your left as you enter, look for a caged display cabinet. A small black-and-white Mickey face (possibly on a ceramic mug) stares back at you from behind a green vase sitting at the left side of the third shelf.

Hint 25: A Mickey-shaped lock is attached to a horizontal valve wheel near the rightmost ride lift on the lower level.

Cars Land

- Luigi's Rollickin' Roadsters

Hint 26: Along the entrance queue, as you enter the second room inside, look for collages on the right wall. Behind glass, in the third collage from the right, a tiny red Lightning McQueen antenna topper has a Mickey hat with ears on its roof. This antenna topper is in the right middle part of the collage, below a white piece of paper on which someone has written "# 121."

Hint 27: In the same room, the fourth glass covered collage from the right has a red car with a sideways classic Mickey headlight. The car is above a sign for Buckingham Palace, in the right middle of the collage.

Hint 28: Also in this fourth collage, near the left upper corner, a green and blue round symbol above two silver gears with red decals looks to be an upside-down classic Mickey. Find it above the word "Paris."

- Mater's Junkyard Jamboree

Hint 29: Three hubcaps form a classic Mickey, tilted to the left, in the entrance queue of *Mater 's Junkyard Jamboree*. As you enter the covered area of the queue, they're above you at the far left corner near the ceiling.

Hint 30: Further along the queue, you can see three barrels inside the ride area that are positioned and proportioned to form a classic Mickey standing upright. A red barrel serves as the "head."

Grizzly Peak

- *Soarin' Around the World*

Hint 31: In the pre-show video, a man is asked to remove his Mickey Mouse ears.

Hint 32: Also in the pre-show, a boy sitting in his ride seat is wearing a shirt with a Grumpy logo and shorts sporting Mickey Mouse.

Hint 33: Early in the film, you'll approach a castle in Germany. Look to the left in the distance at a footbridge that crosses a chasm. To the right of the far end of the footbridge, a black classic Mickey marking is on the edge of the hill at about the same level as the bridge.

Hint 34: In the scene with hot air balloons floating above the desert, three colorful balloons in the distance merge together as a classic Hidden Mickey. The image is visible for only a few seconds.

Hint 35: When you approach the round Fiji island, focus on the beach right in front of you. Three small rocks near the lower right edge of the beach come together as a classic Mickey, tilted slightly to the left.

Hint 36: As you fly over Disneyland's Main Street, U. S.A. near the end of the ride, some people walking below you are carrying Mickey balloons.

Hint 37: As you approach Sleeping Beauty Castle, watch for a classic Mickey made of bursts of white fireworks over the Castle.

- [*Soarin' Over California*

Hint 38: In the pre-show video, a man is asked to remove his Mickey Mouse ears.

Hint 39: Also in the pre-show, a boy sitting in his ride seat is wearing a shirt with a Grumpy logo and shorts sporting Mickey Mouse.

Hint 40: When you soar over the hills and spot a golf course, look immediately to your lower left and find a golf cart. The man standing on the other side of the cart is holding a blue Mickey balloon.

Hint 41: Now look fast to the right side of the golf course. About halfway along the fairway, a slightly distorted classic Mickey shadow is cast on the green grass by a cluster of three trees. The "ears" of the shadow Mickey touch the right side of the white cart path.

Hint 42: Stare straight ahead and down to the golf course. Spot the man about to swing a golf club. When he strikes the golf ball, it will head directly toward you. Don't blink! Watch the ball's rotation to see the dark classic Mickey on the surface of the ball.

Hint 43: As you fly over Disneyland's Main Street, U. S.A. near the end of the ride, some people walking below you are carrying Mickey balloons.

Hint 44: As you approach Sleeping Beauty Castle, watch for a classic Mickey made of bursts of white fireworks over the Castle.]

Hollywood Land

- Disney Junior Dance Party!

Hint 45: Small classic Mickeys appear and disappear on the main screen during the live show.

Hint 46: In the front leftmost outside window of the *Disney Junior Dance Party* building, facing the street, is a display for "Mickey and the Roadster Racers" (a Disney children's TV show). Several small classic Mickey patches can be spotted on Mickey and Minnie, along with several larger decorative (not hidden) classic Mickey images.

Buena Vista Street

- Five & Dime show
Hint 47: The tires on the *Five & Dime show* vehicle have classic Mickeys in the tread.

Hollywood Land

- Disney Animation Building

Hint 48: A small classic Mickey sits atop the flagpole over the front of the *Animation Building*.

Hint 49: Along the top of some outside windows and wall pillars, classic Mickey "hats" are in the tile design.

Hint 50: A drum set shaped like a classic Mickey sits on a shelf high above the stage inside the *Animation Academy*.

Hint 51: A red classic Mickey-shaped picture frame is on the top shelf at the middle of the Animator's desk on the left side of the stage. (You'll also find many decorative Mickey images on and around the stage.)

Hint 52: Side-profile Mickeys (a bit abstract) are repeated in the pattern of the stage carpet. (Be aware that carpets are changed from time to time).

Hint 53: In the *Sorcerer's Workshop* area, Sorcerer Mickey is on the left wall toward the end of the room. He's encircled by classic Mickey bubbles. Nearby on the left wall, you'll find a classic Mickey intertwined with the middle of a treble clef.

Hint 54: In the *Beast's Library*, just past the Sorcerer's Workshop, a classic Mickey design is in the upper middle of the grate in front of a faux fireplace.

Hint 55: In the mosaic lettering on the exit walls, large and small circles form many classic Mickeys.

Hint 56: The shadow of a person with Mickey ears appears at the bottom of the "Character Close-up" poster on the wall outside.

- Off the Page shop

Hint 57: In an outside display window of the shop, the last of several Dalmatians has an upside-down classic Mickey made of spots on its rear thigh.

Hint 58: On a drawing hanging from the ceiling in the middle of *Off the Page*, bubbles form a classic Mickey in front of the shadow of an alligator's front leg.

- Schmoozies

Hint 59: Face *Schmoozies* from the street,

and then walk to the left side of the store. There are two murals on the left wall. The one on the right has classic Mickeys formed by small round green and white pieces of colored glass.

Hint 60: Now face the shop from Hollywood Boulevard. A classic Mickey formed by three tan stones hides to the right of a knife tip and above a pink cup on the right side of the rightmost mural on the front of the shop.

Hint 61: Near the center of the mosaic mural closest to Fairfax Market, a red jewel with two button ears forms a classic Mickey. It's to the right of the word "EAT."

Hint 62: On the rear wall directly behind the front smoothie order windows, a Hidden Minnie Mouse decked out as the Statue of Liberty is in the middle and near the top of the wall mosaic.

Pixar Pier

- Incredicoaster

Hint 63: When you're upside down in the loop, look at the ground to your left for a classic Mickey cement footing at the base of one of the vertical support poles. You can also spot this Mickey if you look right as you ride through the little hills that cover the *Toy Story Midway Mania!* attraction building.

Grizzly Peak

- Redwood Creek Challenge Trail

Hint 64: You'll find three classic Mickeys on the left side of the trail map. A group of three rocks in a stream forms a Hidden Mickey at the top left of the map. Three circles in the middle left form a classic Mickey in foam (look just to the left of the mouth of the left water slide). Lower down, three log seats in the Ahwahnee Camp Circle are arranged to create a classic Mickey.

Hint 65: Climb the stairs to the Mt. Whitney Lookout and check out the phonetic spelling alphabet (also known as the NATO phonetic alphabet and more accurately as the International Radiotelephony Spelling Alphabet) on a sheet of paper atop a table in the Lookout room. The word for "M" in the official phonetic spelling alphabet is "Mike." But this is Disney! So, the word for "M" is, you guessed it – "Mickey"!

- Rushin' River Outfitters shop

Hint 66: On some of the stuffed grizzly bears, the rear pads on the bottoms of the paws are shaped like classic Mickeys.

- Near Grizzly River Run entrance

Hint 67: A classic Mickey made of rocks is embedded in the pavement under the right side of the fence, close to the "Grizzly Peak Recreation Area" cabin.

Paradise Gardens Park

- The Little Mermaid - Ariel's Undersea Adventure

Hint 68: Classic Mickey circles hide in the design of the ironwork along the sides of the upper support for the entrance queue cover.

Hint 69: As you enter the queue inside the building, the globes in the chandeliers merge together from certain vantage points to form classic Mickeys.

Hint 70: As you approach the loading dock area along the entrance queue, you pass under an arch with an orange scallop shell painted on it. Two gold scepters project from the top of the shell. Three light green circles just above the top middle of the shell come together as an upside-down classic Mickey.

Hint 71: A small classic Mickey is impressed in a large rock at the lower left corner of the loading dock mural, just above the green tile. You can spot this Hidden Mickey from the entrance queue and again as you pass by it on your right in your seashell vehicle.

Hint 72: During the first part of the ride, Scuttle the seagull sits to the left of a wooden crate. A keyring hanging over the edge of the crate has several metal circles that form a classic Hidden Mickey at certain angles. (This image seems to change shape at times).

Hint 73: Just before you enter the room where the song "Under the Sea" is playing, a collection of purple coral appears to your left above some starfish on a brown rock outcropping. A classic Mickey is formed by three holes on the upper part of the top round coral.

Hint 74: In the same room, three pink spots near the middle of the spinning purple octopus's head form a sideways classic Mickey, tilted to the right.

Hint 75: As you approach the singing Ariel, stare at the standing tubular coral stalks below her. In the middle of the group of corals, the round tops of three stalks form a classic Mickey tilted to the right.

Hint 76: Just past Ariel, watch for a green fish with a tall purple turban hat who is dancing with Flounder (the yellow and blue fish). This green fish has a large, oval yellow earring on her left ear, and at the top of the earring is a small, blue classic Mickey.

Hint 77: As soon as you pass Flounder, look quickly over your right shoulder - across the track from Flounder - for a blue Hidden Mr. Limpet (Don Knotts as a fish from "The Incredible Mr. Limpet" movie). He's wearing glasses and peeking out from the green seaweed. (Not a Hidden Mickey, but a cool Hidden Surprise!)

Hint 78: Toward the end of the ride, check the pond (to your right) for frogs with dark spots on their backs that form sideways classic Mickeys.

Hint 79: To the rear left of the boat with Ariel and Eric and behind the frogs and fish, three lily pads form a classic Mickey on the water.

Hint 80: Another Hidden Surprise – a Hidden Tribute - awaits you at the end of the ride, right before you exit your clam-mobile. In a small recess in the wall to your left, silhouettes on dark brown cabinet doors outline Hans Christian Andersen (on the door to the left) and The Little Mermaid statue in Copenhagen, Denmark (on the door to the right). "The Little Mermaid" was one of the fairy tales written by Danish author Hans Christian Andersen.

Pacific Wharf

-Walt Disney Imagineering Blue Sky Cellar

Hint 81: Just inside the front door, a cloud side profile of the body of Sorcerer Mickey is at the lower left of the blue entrance sign on the wall.

Hint 82: Go inside and turn back into the center area. In the left middle of the display on the left (as you face the main entrance), three small paint containers come together as a classic Mickey.

Hint 83: You'll find other Mickey images in the displays on the left and right, including a Mickey mug and Mickey clocks.

Hint 84: Along an outside walkway behind *Blue Sky Cellar*, three grapes in a painting of white wine grapes form a classic Mickey on the left branch at the upper left of a group of Pinot Grigio grapes.

Cars Land

- Cozy Cone Motel

Hint 85: Inside the *Cozy Cone Motel* office, Buzz Lightyear peeks out from under an orange cone on a shelf at the end of a counter. He can be spotted from a rear window of the office, which is locked and closed to guests. A Hidden Mickey figurine is on the lower shelf at the other end (the front) of the counter. (Note: At times, you may spot other Hidden Characters on these shelves.)

- Residents of Radiator Springs Greeting Area

Hint 86: The wing nut on Mater's engine air filter has Mickey ears.

- Radiator Springs Curios Store

Hint 87: On the far left lower wall of the front porch of *Radiator Springs Curios Store*, a classic Mickey is on the upper right outer edge of a yellow "Pump" sign. (Note: Sometimes this sign is partially hidden by furniture or other objects on the porch.)

Hint 88: Inside the store, on the wall to the right of the cashier, a yellow "Service" sign and two round red hubcaps form a classic Mickey.

Hint 89: Some groups of circles on the ceiling inside the store form classic Mickeys.

- Ramone's House of Body Art store

Hint 90: In the rightmost outside display window of *Ramone's House of Body Art*, a small white classic Mickey, tilted to the right, lies in a light yellow square area about halfway up the right side of the car hood.

Hint 91: In a nearby window, spot a car hood with orange and yellow "flames." A faint classic Mickey hides on the far right side of the hood under the rightmost blue vertical streak.

Hint 92: In the next window, a tiny white classic Hidden Mickey is at the middle bottom of a brown car hood with a pinstripe design. You have to look very low to see this one!

Hint 93: Moving to your left, another car hood hosts a faint white classic Mickey. It's on the right side, in the bottom red fringe of the second blue-and-red vertical design from the right.

Hint 94: In the second outside display window from the far left, a subtle white classic Mickey hides in the red flame in the lower middle of a bronze and white car hood. It's in a trough of the flame just to the right of midline. This Hidden Mickey is very hard to spot!

Hint 95: In the outside display window at the far left of the storefront, a white classic Mickey is in the lacy fabric at the lower middle of a car hood.

Hint 96: Inside the store, a faint white classic Mickey is on the right side of a purple car hood that stands behind the front sales counter. It's just above and to the far right of the word "Ramone's."

Hint 97: Classic Mickeys are part of the decorative pinstripe design on the support pillars inside Ramone's.

Hint 98: Subtle classic Mickeys are traced on a few paint-splattered boxes on the floor and on shelves inside the store.

- Near the Fire Department building

Hint 99: A sideways classic Mickey is high up on a power line that hangs on a telephone pole to the left of the statue of Stanley the car, near the *Town of Radiator Springs Fire Department building*.

Pacific Wharf

- The Bakery Tour

Hint 100: On a table in a corner of the first room, you'll see bread rolls. Sometimes they're shaped like Mickey; other times they're imprinted with him.

Pixar Pier

- Jessie's Critter Carousel

Hint 101: On the blue armadillo in the outer circle, a classic Mickey made of spots sits on the right front shoulder area.

- Jack-Jack Cookie Num Nums

Hint 102: At the rear of the cookie stand is a mural that shows Jack-Jack holding a cookie that has three chocolate chips shaped as a classic Mickey.

- Along the promenade

Hint 103: One of the billboards along the promenade between Incredicoaster and the Adorable Snowman Frosted Treats shop is titled "Keep Our Pier Clean." On the left side of the poster, baby otters are holding a plastic six-pack can holder. The reflection of the six-pack holder in the water reveals an upside-down classic Mickey.

Paradise Gardens Park

- Seaside Souvenirs shop

Hint 104: Look for one or more Mickey balloons painted high on the walls behind merchandise shelves inside the shop.

Hint 105: Two brown Nautilus submarines are also painted behind the shelves. (Note: "Nautilus" is the submarine, commanded by Captain Nemo, in Jules Verne's novel *Twenty Thousand Leagues Under the Sea*.)

Hollywood Land

- *Mickey's PhilharMagic*

Hint 106: In the "Be Our Guest" portion of the movie, there is a point where you are watching Lumiere dancing on the table with other characters. The view goes to an overhead shot and there are shadows cast on the table from the candle hands of Lumiere. These shadows come together at times to form what appear to be Hidden Mickeys.

Hint 107: In "The Little Mermaid" segment, Ariel throws jewels out into the water in front of her. Focus on the gold ring to the right (your right) of Ariel. A dark classic Mickey is visible just as you first spot the open center of the ring as it starts rotating. The center hole in the ring becomes round – not Mickey-shaped – as the ring completes its rotation.

Hint 108: Watch closely as Aladdin and Jasmine ride their magic carpet in the sky. Stare at the bottom left of the screen for a quick glimpse of three buildings on the ground. Their bright domes are clustered together as a classic Mickey. The lower dome sits in a larger round dark circle to form the "head" of the Hidden Mickey.

Buena Vista Street

- 1901 Lounge

Hint 109: A tiny white classic Hidden Mickey hides in the white tile in front of the entrance door to the *1901 Lounge* next to the entrance to *Carthay Circle Restaurant*.

- Clarabelle's Hand-Scooped Ice Cream Shop

Hint 110: Along a rear wall inside the shop, the cows on the Clarabelle's Dairy Milk bottles displayed behind the counter have classic Mickey spots on their sides.

- Julius Katz & Sons store

Hint 111: In an outside display window of the store, a classic Mickey image is on a test pattern on a television screen.

Hint 112: Inside the store, a classic Mickey image is formed by the ends of rollers on a small silver mechanical device, which sits on a top shelf along a wall at the rear.

- Big Top Toys store

Hint 113: Inside the store, a gray classic Hidden Mickey, tilted to the right, hides on the dapple horse at the lower middle of the mural behind the cashier's counter. The Hidden Mickey is located on the right side of the horse's neck, just above the decorative orange reins.

- near Oswald's

Hint 114: On a wall above and to the right of the Chamber of Commerce building near *Oswald's*, a blue painted advertisement says "Elias and Company, Open 7 Days." A tiny white classic Mickey hides along the inner border of the blue area, to the right of the "N" in "Open."

- Buena Vista Street Trolley Station

Hint 115: At the trolley station waiting area near the main park entrance, a classic Mickey made of rocks hides in the support pillar nearest the park entrance. It's under the four vertical red bricks, which are at the top of the outer right side of the pillar nearest the street. This Hidden Mickey is tilted to the left, and the left "ear" has striped markings.

Main Entrance Plaza

Hint 116: Ironwork gratings surround some tree trunks in the entrance plaza. Tiny classic Mickey fasteners hold a few of the ironwork bands in place.

Hint 117: You'll find classic Mickey holes inside the braces that support the plaza's ticket-booth counters.

Paradise Bay

- World of Color

Hint 118: Watch for the *Up* scene on the water screen during the World of Color show. Just as the *Up* house floats off the screen, a Mickey balloon soars up and speeds after the house.

Notes

Chapter 4

Downtown Disney District & Resort Hotel Scavenger Hunt

Because you may want to hunt only one area at a time, I've listed the perfect score for each area in parentheses after its name in the Clues section.

Downtown Disney District
(11 points)

* Begin your Downtown Disney search at the entrance across from the *Disneyland Hotel* at about 11:00 a.m. (Note: Disney may close one or more of the Downtown Disney stores mentioned below to make way for new experiences).

* Enter **Splitsville Luxury Lanes**.

Clue 1: Locate a Hidden Mickey near the bowling lanes on the lower level.
3 points

Clue 2: Now search the upper level walls for a classic Hidden Mickey.
3 points

* Your next stop is **Marceline's Confectionery**.

Clue 3: Find a Hidden Mickey outside the store.
3 points

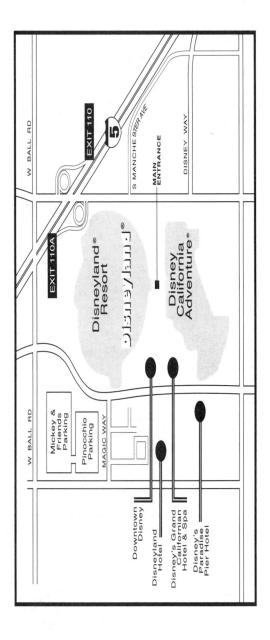

Clue 4: Study the **kiosks** near the entrance plaza.
2 points

*
Now head for the **Mickey & Friends Parking Structure** to find more Hidden Mickeys. You can walk there or take a tram from Downtown Disney.

Mickey & Friends Parking Structure
(17 points)

Clue 5: Stop and look up at the directional sign on the walkway near the tram stop.
2 points

Clue 6: Inside the parking structure, walk up to Level 2 (Daisy Level) and find a Hidden Mickey between poles 3A and 3B.
5 points

Clue 7: Now search near pole 2A.
4 points

Clue 8: While still inside the parking structure, walk to the front of the parking level to spot a Hidden Mickey on a sign. (Psst: It's posted on an entrance car ramp.)
4 points

Hop on the tram to the parks.
Clue 9: Spot Mickey on a pole.
2 points

*
Make your way back to Downtown Disney, then walk over to **Disney's Grand Californian Hotel & Spa**.

Disney's Grand Californian Hotel & Spa
(85 points)

*
Look around outside the main entrance.

Clue 10: Search for Mickey's full face on a panel.
5 points

Clue 11: In this same area, find classic Mickeys on four different panels.
5 points for four or more

*
Now enter the lobby.
Clue 12: Search low for a Hidden Mickey.
3 points

Clue 13: Study the front of the main registration counters for a "conductor Mickey."
5 points

Clue 14: Now search the front of these registration counters nearby for a classic Mickey.
4 points

Clue 15: Finally, search the front of the registration counters one last time for a Hidden Tinker Bell.
5 points

Clue 16: Glance behind the main registration counters for a classic Mickey on a tree.
4 points

Clue 17: Look for two other classic Mickeys behind the main registration counters.
4 points for finding both

Clue 18: Search the other registration counter at the far left (as you face the main registration counter) for three Hidden Mickeys.
5 points for finding all three

Clue 19: Ask a Cast Member at one of the lobby counters to show you a "Disney's Grand Californian Hotel & Spa" writing pen. Study it for a Hidden Mickey!
5 points

Clue 20: This Hidden Mickey knows what time it is!
5 points

Clue 21: Spot a Mickey image on a desk.
3 points

Clue 22: Locate Hidden Mickeys on telephones.
2 points for spotting two or more

Clue 23: Find Mickey on a map.
3 points

Clue 24: Look for Mickey on a wall in the hallway with the restrooms not far from the registration counters.
3 points

Clue 25: Search for Mickey near the fireplace.
3 points

Clue 26: Just outside the exit doors near and to the rear of the fireplace is a Hidden Mickey similar to the one ab ove!
3 points

* Enter the **_Hearthstone Lounge_**.

Clue 27: Check around for a Hidden Mickey.
2 points

If you're hungry, snack inside Hearthstone Lounge or try to get seated for lunch at Storytellers Cafe.

*
Stroll through the exit doors that lead to *Downtown Disney*.

Clue 28: Look up and to your right for a Hidden Mickey.
3 points

*
Return to the main lobby and take the exit that leads to *Disney California Adventure Park*.

Clue 29: After a few steps, look up for Mickey.
3 points

Clue 30: Now locate Mickey close to the walkway.
2 points

Clue 31: Walk to the **Mandara Spa** to find Hidden Disney Characters.
4 points

*
Head back to the Grand Californian lobby once more and stroll out the front entrance to Disneyland Drive (which will take you over to *Disney's Paradise Pier Hotel* if you are up for more Mickey hunting now).

Clue 32: Find Mickey on a sign.
2 points

Clue 33: Search for Mickey bike racks.
2 points

*
When you are ready to continue your Mickey sleuthing, stroll over to **Disney's Paradise Pier Hotel**.

Disney's Paradise Pier Hotel
(35 points)

Clue 34: Spot Mickey on a wall outside
the front entrance of the hotel.
4 points

*
Step inside the hotel.

Clue 35: Study a painting in the lobby
for a Hidden Mickey.
4 points

Clue 36: Find a telephone nearby for
another Hidden Mickey.
2 points

Clue 37: Spot Mickey near the fitness
center and the Beachcomber Club.
4 points for finding both

Clue 38: Look inside the elevators for
classic Mickeys.
2 points for two or more

Clue 39: Find a Hidden Mickey near the
elevators.
2 points

Clue 40: Mickey is near the swimming
pool.
2 points

*
Search for classic Mickeys in **Disney's
PCH Grill restaurant**.

Clue 41: Study the carpet. (Carpets may
be changed at times).
2 points

Clue 42: Search for Mickeys of different
sizes in the wall decor.
3 points for finding both sizes

Clue 43: Look for Mickey on lamps.
2 points

Clue 44: Search for three camouflaged Mickeys on three separate surfboards.
5 points for sleuthing out all three

Clue 45: Find two Mickeys on entrance doors.
2 points for spotting both

* Search outside the hotel's rear entrance.

Clue 46: You can't miss Mickey outside the first-floor rear entrance.
1 point

* Gaze south from an upper floor.

Clue 47: If you can access an upper floor to look south along Disneyland Drive, you might be able to make out two sidewalks that outline a classic Mickey. (Or, zoom into the image on Google Earth).
5 bonus points

* Your final stop: the *Disneyland Hotel*.

Disneyland Hotel
(59 points)

* Check out the area outside the front entrance.

Clue 48: Spot Hidden Mickeys in the nearby parking lot.
1 point

Clue 49: While you're at the hotel entrance, don't miss Mickey on the luggage carts.
1 point

* Step into the lobby.
Clue 50: Search for tiny Hidden Mickeys in the registration lobby.
3 points

Clue 51: Find Mickey facing the main lobby elevators.
3 points

Clue 52: Study the mirrored glass walls inside the elevators for Mickey.
3 points

*
Return to the main lobby.

Clue 53: Study nearby telephones for Hidden Mickeys.
2 points

*
Now look around the hotel complex to find more Hidden Mickeys.

Clue 54: Spot a Hidden Mickey in the **Convention Center** area.
2 points

Clue 55: Search the ceiling near **Goofy's Kitchen** for Hidden Mickeys.
5 points for five Hidden Mickeys

Clue 56: Don't overlook Mickey on the stair handrail!
1 point

Clue 57: Look up for two Mickey images above the top of a staircase.
4 points for both

Clue 58: Upstairs from *Goofy's Kitchen*, find a painting of Toontown on the wall and study it to spot two Hidden Mickeys.
4 points for finding both

Clue 59: In a painting nearby of a *Splash Mountain* scene, look for three Hidden Mickeys.
5 points for spotting all three

Clue 60: Locate a painting of *Space Mountain*. It has a Hidden Mickey, too!
3 points

Clue 61: Stroll the hotel hallways near the Sleeping Beauty Pavilion for Hidden Mickeys at your feet.
2 points for one or more

Clue 62: Near the Sleeping Beauty Pavilion, scrutinize a painting of a jungle temple for a Hidden Mickey.
5 points

*
Walk into the **Frontier Tower** lobby.

Clue 63: Find furniture in a Mickey shape.
2 points

Clue 64: In the lobby, search for a tiny classic Mickey in a display.
5 points

Clue 65: Near the *Frontier Tower* lobby, locate classic Mickeys on a dress.
4 points

Clue 66: Also near the lobby, look for a painting with two Mickey hats.
4 points for both

Time now to see how you did.

Total Points for Downtown Disney and the Resort Hotels =

How'd You Do?

Up to 83 points - Bronze
84 to 166 points - Silver
167 points and over - Gold
207 points - Perfect Score

You may have done even better if you
earned bonus points with the sidewalk
Hidden Mickey on Disneyland Drive.

Notes

If you need help, the Hints are here for you!

Downtown Disney District

(Note: Disney may close one or more of the Downtown Disney stores mentioned below to make way for new experiences).

- Splitsville Luxury Lanes

Hint 1: Inside *Splitsville Luxury Lanes*, look around the lower level for a classic Hidden Mickey on the wall. It's formed of holes in a large orange in a mural – entitled "Welcome to Golden Lanes" – painted on the wall on the right of the bowling lanes.

133

Hint 2: Another classic Hidden Mickey is at the lower left of an upper level mural – entitled "Greetings from Splitsville @ Downtown Disney District" – and is made by finger holes in a brown bowling ball.

- *Marceline's Confectionery*

Hint 3: On the sign in front of the store, swirls in the letters "M" and "C" combine to form a classic Mickey.

- *Kiosks near the entrance plaza*

Hint 4: The eaves of several kiosks sport classic Mickey-shaped supports.

Mickey & Friends Parking Structure

- *Walkway near the tram stop*

Hint 5: On the walkway near the tram stop, a classic Mickey sits atop the sign that points the way to *Mickey & Friends Parking Structure*.

- *Inside the parking structure*

Hint 6: A classic Mickey is etched in the cement midway between poles 3A and 3B, next to an unnumbered pole and under an "Emergency" sign.

Hint 7: A classic Mickey is etched in the cement two car stalls over from pole 2A, as you head toward the exit drive path.

Hint 8: Look for a yellow sign on a wall at one end of an automobile entrance ramp at the side of the walkway to the Trams. A classic Mickey is at the top of a "Caution - U-Turn" sign.

- Tram to the parks

Hint 9: Classic Mickeys top the light poles that line the tram path from the *Mickey & Friends Parking Structure* to the parks. (You can spot these light pole Mickeys in other areas around the Disneyland Resort property, such as in some of the parking lots.)

Disney's Grand Californian Hotel & Spa

- Outside the main entrance

Hint 10: A pillar just outside the main entrance is covered with colorful panels. On the rear panel, a three - quarter image of Mickey's face looks out from between the outer branches of a tree. He's about three quarters of the way up the left side of the tree.

Hint 11: On this same rear panel, a classic Mickey is at the middle bottom of the tree, just above the trunk. A second classic Mickey is in another tree at the upper right of the panel. In fact, you can spot small classic Mickeys in some of the trees on all four panels around this pillar!

- Lobby area and nearby hallways

Hint 12: As you enter the *Grand Californian* lobby, look for a rug with the hotel's tree logo to spot the small classic Mickey above the tree's trunk. (Wherever you come across the *Grand Californian Hotel* logo, you're likely to spot a classic Mickey in the lower middle of the tree branches.)

Hint 13: A small side view of Mickey Mouse is sculpted in tile on the front desk. Toward the middle of the long counter, look for dancing bears on a panel in a depression in the desk. Mickey Mouse is conducting with a wand to the right of the white bear.

Hint 14: To the right of "conductor Mickey" is a raised, brown and green classic Mickey on the lower middle part of a tree.

Hint 15: To the left of "conductor Mickey" is a figure of Tinker Bell near (and to the immediate left of) a flat, dark writing surface.

Hint 16: On a fabric mural on the far left side of the rear wall behind the main registration counters, a dark classic Mickey hides just above the trunk in the branches of the leftmost tree.

Hint 17: You can spot two classic Mickeys on the left side of a fabric mural that hangs on the far right side of the rear wall behind the main registration counters. One is below the second maroon line from the top and the other is above the fifth maroon line from the top.

Hint 18: On the registration counter to the far left (as you face the main registration counters), look for ceramic green trees on each side of the front of the counter. Classic Mickeys are in their lower branches. A third classic Mickey sits in the lower middle branches of a tiny light-yellow tree to the upper left of the green tree on the right side of the counter.

Hint 19: Disneyland Resort's smallest Hidden Mickey is on a writing pen labeled with "Disney's Grand Californian Hotel & Spa." The tiny classic Mickey is on the tree logo for the hotel, at the bottom middle of the tree limbs.

Hint 20: A classic Mickey depression is on the face of the grandfather clock in the main lobby.

Hint 21: A classic Mickey hole is in the middle front of a desk, high up under the projecting lip of the desktop. The desk is usually at the rear left of the main lobby.

Hint 22: Telephones near the lobby elevators sport two classic Mickeys each, one above a touchtone button at the lower part of the phone information panel and another at the top of the panel in the tree logo for the *Grand Californian Hotel*.

Hint 23: On a map of the *Grand Californian* on a wall along a walkway at the left (as you enter) of the main lobby, the Children's Pool area is shaped like a classic Mickey.

Hint 24: In the nearby hallway to the left of the main entrance (as you face in from the entrance), classic Mickeys are in the corners of the frame of a painting that hangs on the wall near the restrooms. The painting shows a rocky and mountainous coastline.

Hint 25: A classic Mickey made of round stones and tilted to the right is in the lower front part of the rock wall on the left side of the lobby fireplace.

Hint 26: Another classic Mickey made of round rocks is in the wall to your right as you walk out the exit doors near and to the rear of the fireplace. A crack crosses Mickey's "head," which is in the second row from the top of the rock pile and four rocks back from the far edge of the wall. The classic Mickey is tilted to the right, almost sideways.

- Hearthstone Lounge

Hint 27: Classic Mickey holes repeat near the outer rim of some of the large light fixtures on the walls and hanging from the ceiling in the *Hearthstone Lounge*.

- Walkway to Downtown Disney

Hint 28: As you start along the walkway to Downtown Disney District, turn to your right and look up to spot a classic Mickey on the *Grand Californian* logo tree in an upper-story window.

- Walkway to Disney California Adventure

Hint 29: The side panels of the lamps along the walkway to the Disney California Adventure Park entrance are embellished with tree designs. The tallest tree on each panel has a classic Mickey at the bottom center of the tree limbs.

Hint 30: Classic Mickeys adorn each of the *Grand Californian* tree logos that are embossed on the planters lining the walkway.

Hint 31: An outside window of the **Mandara Spa** shows a forest scene. Silhouettes of Bambi and his father stand near the bottom of the window. A bench in front of the window often hides the two deer.

- Disneyland Drive

Hint 32: The large *Grand Californian* entrance signs facing Disneyland Drive include the hotel's tree logo with its classic Mickey.

Hint 33: As you face the *Grand Californian Hotel* from Disneyland Drive, look for a Cast Member entrance driveway to the right of the main entrance to the hotel. Bicycle racks shaped as classic Mickeys are along the left side of this driveway.

Disney's Paradise Pier Hotel

- *Outside the front entrance*

Hint 34: Classic Mickey impressions are in the gray recessed wall just to the left of the front entrance (as you face the hotel).

- *Inside the hotel*

Hint 35: A large painting hangs on a wall facing the main entrance. In the painting's upper right, a black classic Mickey tilted to the right hides inside a red cart on a Ferris wheel. (It might be Mickey himself!)

Hint 36: Telephones near the central lobby sport a classic Mickey above one of the touchtone buttons along the bottom.

Hint 37: On the second floor, you'll find classic Mickey wooden cutouts in the trim of the entrance doors to both Mickey's Fitness Center and the Beach Comber Club. (An entrance door to Mickey's Fitness Center also features a large decorative classic-Mickey window.)

Hint 38: Classic Mickeys are scattered in the colorful designs of surfboards on the inside elevator walls.

Hint 39: White classic Mickeys appear in the dark blue guest hallway carpets. (Note: Carpets change from time to time, but you can usually find Hidden Mickeys in any new carpets in the hotels.)

Hint 40: On the third floor, classic Mickeys grace the top railings around the swimming pool.

- Disney's PCH Grill

Hint 41: A multicolored classic Mickey in swirls is woven into the restaurant's carpet.

Hint 42: Small black classic Mickeys hide on diagonal wires on the wall, while a large, black partial classic Mickey hides higher up on the wall near the kitchen.

Hint 43: Black classic Mickeys are on the food lamps hanging in the kitchen area.

Hint 44: Three different surfboards decorating the restaurant's walls shelter classic Mickeys, one in fireworks, one in Rowers, and one in black circles at the bottom of the surfboard.

Hint 45: Black partial classic Mickeys hide in the glass panels of each of the double doors at the PHC Grill's entrance.

- Outside the rear entrance

Hint 46: Classic Mickeys are atop short poles just outside the rear entrance to the hotel.

- From Upper Floors

Hint 47: This classic Mickey takes its

shape from two sidewalks on either side of Disneyland Drive approaching Katella Avenue. The sidewalks themselves provide the outline, and you can really only see it from above. Trees planted near the sidewalks may obscure the image from overhead. You might be able to spot the image from upper floors in *Paradise Pier Hotel*. Otherwise, you can admire it from the air or on Google Earth.

Disneyland Hotel

- *Lobby and entrance areas*

Hint 48: Classic Mickeys top the light poles in the main entrance parking lot.

Hint 49: Classic Mickeys are hiding in the middle of the side railings of the luggage carts.

Hint 50: In the lobby, several blue rectangular panels decorate the front of the long registration counter. These panels contain many tiny bubbles of different sizes that form classic Mickeys at intervals.

Hint 51: A wall covered with photographs faces the main lobby elevators. Above right of the large photo of Walt Disney with a map of Disneyland is a photo of Walt leaning out of a train; he's holding a large Mickey doll.

Hint 52: On the mirrored glass on the left side wall of the elevators (as you face the doors from inside), a small white classic Mickey hides in the stars near the elevator doors.

Hint 53: Back upstairs, the telephones in the hallways near the central lobby sport classic Mickeys above one of the touchtone buttons at the bottom of the phones.

- Around the hotel complex

Hint 54: Inside the hotel, in the *Convention Center* area to the right, you can usually flnd classic Hidden Mickeys in the carpet.

Hint 55: To the right of *Goofy's Kitchen* and *Steakhouse 55,* umbrellas hanging from the ceiling sport classic Hidden Mickeys.

Hint 56: Gold classic Mickeys are atop the ends of the middle handrail on the stairs near *Goofy's Kitchen.*

Hint 57: On the ceiling at the top of a staircase near *Goofy's Kitchen*, a large classic Mickey on a blue background is secured by small classic Mickey bolts.

Hint 58: Find the woman wearing a red dress in the right lower section of a stylized painting of Toontown. The two children with her are wearing Mickey ears.

Hint 59: Look at the lower right section of the painting of a scene in front of *Splash Mountain*. From left to right, you can spot three classic Mickeys: a red Mickey balloon, a small white and black Mickey balloon, and, at the far right of the painting, a child with Mickey ears.

Hint 60: Glance around for a painting of *Space Mountain*. In the sky at the upper left is a fireworks classic Mickey tilted to the left.

- *Near Sleeping Beauty Pavilion*

Hint 61: Classic Mickeys are in the carpet in the hallways near the Sleeping Beauty Pavilion and the Magic Kingdom Ballroom.

Hint 62: Across from the Sleeping Beauty Pavilion, a classic Mickey hides in a painting of a jungle temple. It's on the top front of the hood of a jeep at the lower middle of the painting.

- *Frontier Tower Lobby*

Hint 63: In the *Frontier Tower* Lobby, ottomans are often arranged in a classic Mickey formation. You'll sometimes find the same arrangement in the *Fantasy and Adventure Towers*.

Hint 64: In the lobby is a miniature concept model of the *Big Thunder Mountain Railroad* attraction in Disneyland. Along the rear side of the display, you can spot the three-gear classic Mickey by the track, representing the real classic Mickey gears on the park ride. The gear Hidden Mickey sits on the ground near a wooden tower.

Hint 65: In a hallway to the left of the lobby, check out the right wall next to the stairwell for a painting of a steamboat landing. In its foreground, a woman walks with two children. Her dress has a classic Mickey pattern.

Hint 66: In the stairwell itself (leading down from the hallway to the left of the Frontier Tower lobby), look for a painting with the word "Frontierland." A child in a train car in the middle of the painting is wearing Mickey ears, as is a man in the stagecoach at the top of the painting.

Notes

Chapter 5

Other Mickey Appearances

These Hidden Mickeys won't earn you any points, but you're bound to enjoy them if you're in the right place at the right time to see them.

Look for holiday Hidden Mickeys if you're at Disneyland during the Christmas season, or for that matter, any major holiday.

Other "Hidden" Mickeys - decor and deliberate - appear with some regularity throughout the Disneyland Resort. Notice the Mickster on Disneyland brochures, maps and flags, Cast Member name tags, Cast Member uniforms, guest room keys, telephones and phone books, and restaurant and store receipts. The restaurants sometimes offer classic Mickey butter and margarine pats, pancakes and waffles, and pizzas and pasta, as well as Mickey napkins. They also arrange dishes and condiments to form classic Mickeys. Some condiment containers are even shaped like Mickey. You might notice classic Mickey holes in the backs of some high chairs. Road signs on Disneyland property may sport Mickey ears, and Disneyland vehicles and monorails may display Mickey Mouse insignia.

Cleaning personnel will often spray the ground, windows, furniture, and other items with three circles of cleaning solution (a classic Mickey) before the final cleansing. Or they may leave three wet Mickey Mouse circles or other Disney character images on the pavement after mopping! Mickey even decorates manhole covers, survey markers, and utility covers in the ground, as you've probably already discovered for yourself.

Enjoy all these Mickeys as you experience Disneyland. And if you want to take some home with you, rest assured that you can always find "Hidden" Mickeys on souvenir mugs, merchandise bags and boxes, T-shirts, and Christmas tree ornaments sold in the Disneyland shops. So even when you're far away from Disneyland, you can continue to enjoy Hidden Mickeys.

To marvel at a Hidden Mickey from above, check out Google Earth and find the classic Mickey created by two sidewalks on either side of Disneyland Drive approaching Katella Avenue--below and just to the right of Disney's Paradise Pier Hotel in the Google Earth image. The sidewalks form a distorted image, but the voters on my website liked it as a Hidden Mickey. I hope you will, too.

To access the image, go to Google Earth (you can download the free Google Earth program), type in "Disneyland, California," and click on the "Search" button next to the destination. Then scroll with your mouse to the left and down until you're just below the Paradise Pier hotel, and you'll see the palm-outlined Hidden Mickey. (The palmlined sidewalks form the head and ears). You may have to play around with the dials on your window to get a good view. (Note: The trees are covering up the image more and more in recent years.)

Notes

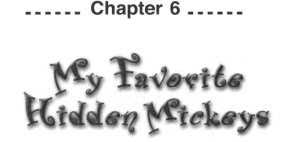

Chapter 6

My Favorite Hidden Mickeys

In this field guide, I've described more than 420 Hidden Mickeys at the Disneyland Resort. I enjoy every one of them, but the following are extra special to me. They're special because of their uniqueness, their deep camouflage (which makes them especially hard to find), or the "Eureka!" response they elicit when I spot them-or any combination of the above. Here then are my Favorite Hidden Mickeys at Disneyland. I apologize to you if your favorite Hidden Mickey is not (yet) on the list below.

My Top Ten

1. Conductor Mickey. Check the registration counter at Disney's Grand Californian Hotel & Spa and marvel at this magnificent (but tiny) rendition of Mickey conducting an imagined musical symphony for the dancing bears nearby. You'll feel like singing along! (Clue 13, Chap. 4)

2. Randall's Mickey. In the *Monster's Inc.* ride, Hollywood Land, Disney California Adventure Park, the little girl Boo pounds monster Randall with a bat. As Randall (who looks like a lizard and changes color like a chameleon) changes colors, a classic Mickey sometimes appears on his belly. This great Mickey image is intermittent, so stare long and

hard at poor Randall, and don't wince!
(Clue 20, Chap. 3)

3. Mountain Snow Mickey, Disneyland
Park. There's more than snow on the
Disneyland Matterhorn! Admire the ma-
jestic mountain from near "it's a small
world" for a Mickey clearing in the snow.
(Clue 12, Chap. 2)

4. Mr. Toad's Door Mickey, Fantasyland, Disneyland Park. You mustn't
miss this marvelous Mickey image on
the right door (lower left corner) of the
third set of doors you crash through at
the beginning of *Mr. Toad's Wild Ride*.
Try not to wreck your car looking for it!
(Clue 35, Chap. 2)

5. 1901 Lounge Doorman Mickey,
Buena Vista Street, Disney California
Adventure. A tiny Mickey below your
feet greets you at the door, wishing
you swell times ahead! (Clue 109,
Chap. 3)

6. Pirate-Armor Mickey, New Orleans
Square, Disneyland. It must've been
one proud pirate who wore this Mickey
armor breastplate which you'll find on
Pirates of the Caribbean. I feel a song
coming on: "Yo, ho, yo, ho, a pirate's life
for me." (Clue 44, Chap. 2)

7. Purple Car-Hood Mickey. This faint
white classic Mickey on a car hood
inside Ramone's House of Body Art in
Cars Land, Disney California Adventure,
is a clever touch by the artist. You may
need help from a Cast Member to find it!
(Clue 96, Chap. 3)

8. Winnie the Pooh's Tree Mickey.
As you take off in your beehive in *The
Many Adventures of Winnie the Pooh*,
Critter Country, Disneyland Park, squint

to your right to admire this subtle classic Mickey in the bark of a tree. When you see it, you'll want to bounce like Tigger! (Clue 127, Chap. 2)

9. Big Ben Mickey. A side view of Mickey's face is below you in a window of Big Ben during *Peter Pan's Flight* in Disneyland's Fantasyland. Look back to spot Mickey in London! (Clue 10, Chap. 2)

10. Mark Twain Mickey. Make a special trip to Frontierland, Disneyland Park, to find a painting of Mickey on a steamboat. He's standing by two well-dressed women on the lower deck of the *Mark Twain Riverboat*. Mickey in a tux! (Clue 70, Chap. 2)

Ten Honorable Mentions

1. Nemo Rock Mickey. Make a special effort to chase down this classic Mickey in a rock wall in Tomorrowland, Disneyland Park, near both the elevator for the *Disneyland Monorail* and *Finding Nemo Submarine Voyage*. You won't regret it! (Clue 78, Chap. 2)

2. Pinocchio Ship Mickey. Pinocchio is a classic, and so is this hard-to-spot, elegant classic Mickey on a model ship's case in *Pinocchio's Daring Journey*, Fantasyland, Disneyland. Ahoy, Mickey! (Clue 144, Chap. 2)

3. *Splash Mountain* Sign Mickey, Critter Country, Disneyland Park. Stop a second and admire this tiny Mickey - it may take your mind off of getting wet! (Clue 74, Chap. 2)

4. Still-life Painting Mickey, Emporium store, Disneyland Park. You may need to step up close to the painting, as this Sorcerer Mickey almost escapes detection! (Clue 175, Chap. 2)

5. Jungle Painting Mickey, Disneyland Hotel. Search this painting on a wall across from the Sleeping Beauty Pavilion for a Hidden Mickey you might encounter while on a wild expedition. (Clue 61, Chap. 4)

6. Lava Mickey. Along the *Toy Story Midway Mania* ride, Pixar Pier, Disney California Adventure, don't overlook Mickey in the lava behind a middle-level balloon. You have to pop the balloon to see Mickey. (Clue 9, Chap. 3)

7. Toontown Dalmatian Mickey. Press the doorbell at the *Fire Department* in Mickey's Toontown in Disneyland, and backpedal to spot a cool Hidden Mickey on the Dalmatian-where else but in its spots! (Clue 123, Chap. 2)

8. *Radiator Springs Racers'* Electrical Mickey, Cars Land, Disney California Adventure. As you motor along, be quick for this Hidden Mickey on an electrical box in Ramone's Body Art shop. Don't worry, if you meet Luigi instead, you can admire Hidden Mickeys behind Luigi and on a red toolbox to your right. (Clue 3, Chap. 3)

9. Schmoozies Minnie. We can't forget Minnie Mouse! At Schmoozies in Disney California Adventure's Hollywood Land, Minnie looks positively regal as the Statue of Liberty. (Clue 62, Chap. 3)

10. Firework Mickey, Mickey's Toontown, Disneyland Park. He's not about to explode, so Mickey will wait patiently for you to smile at him on the outside of the *Fireworks Factory*. (Clue 124, Chap. 2)

Don't Stop Now! ......

Hidden Mickey mania is contagious. The benign pastime of searching out Hidden Mickeys has escalated into a bona fide vacation mission for many Disneyland fans. I'm happy to add my name to the list of hunters. Searching for images of the Main Mouse can enhance a solo trip to the parks or a vacation for the entire family. Little ones delight in spotting and greeting Mickey Mouse characters in the parks and restaurants. As children grow, the Hidden Mickey game is a natural evolution of their fondness for the Mouse.

Join the search! With alert eyes and mind, you can spot Hidden Mickey classics and new ones waiting to be found. Even beginners can happen upon a new, unreported Hidden Mickey or two. As new attractions open and older ones get refurbished, new Hidden Mickeys await discovery.

The Disney entertainment phenomenon is unique in many ways, and Hidden Mickey mania is one manifestation of Disney's universal appeal. Join in the fun! Maybe I'll see you at Disneyland, marveling (like me) at the Hidden Gems. They're waiting patiently for you to discover them.

Notes

Acknowledgements .....

No Hidden Mickey hunter works alone. While I've spotted most of the Hidden Mickeys in this book on my own--and personally verified every single one of them--finding Hidden Mickeys is an ongoing group effort. I am indebted to the following dedicated Hidden Mickey explorers for alerting me to a number of Hidden Mickeys I might otherwise have missed. Thanks to each and every one of you for putting me on the track of one or more of these Disneyland treasures and, in some cases, also helping me verify them.

Those named in bold letters have spotted 10 or more, which includes current as well as lost Hidden Mickeys.

Extra special thanks to Rosemary and Neil (FindingMickey.com) for spotting and helping me verify over 200 Hidden Mickeys at Disneyland **and to Sharon Dale and Sharon Gee** for finding over 50.

Karlos Aguilera, Jonathan Agurcia, Kala'i Ahlo-Souza, The Alberti's, David Almanza, Kirsty Alsop, Antonio Altamirano, James Amato, Bob Anderson, Katrina Andrews, A.J. Apellido, Issac Aragon, Vahe Arevshatian, Cheryl Armstrong, John Axtell, Kristi B., Ori B., **Brian Babcock, Kim Bacon and Family,** Duane Baker, Jennifer Baker, Ruby Beatrice Baker, Hans Balders, Matt and Shelly and Keira Barbieri, Andrew Bardsley, Katharine and Ammon Barney, Daniel Barrach, Melissa Barrett, Melisa Beardslee, Bradly Behmer, **April Beisser,** Richard Beltran, John Benavidez II, Daniel and Elise Berdin,

Brian Bergstrom, Dessa Bernabe, Jenny Bigpond, **Murray Bishop,** Tina Blaylock, Tyler and Brandie Bolton, Tim Bonanno, Cam Bondoc, Jacob Steven Bonillas, Corey Borgen, Lynn Boyd, Lori Brackett, Chad Bradbury, Erik Bratlien, Vicky Braun, David Breede, Rod Brouhard, Carol Brown, Kaden Brown, Keller Brown, Nicolas Brown, Peter Brown, Thierry and Gabriella and Matthieu Bruxelle, Colin Buchanan, Michael Buell, Fernando Bueno, Josh Burch, Marjorie Burns, Felix Bustos, Nate Buteyn, Amy C., Peter C., Ashley Cabrera, Chris Caflisch, Bev Cain, Stacy Campbell, Craig Canady, Marisa Cardenas, Nicholas Noah Carreno, Peter Cefalu, Gail Chambers, Leonard Chan, Austin Chanu, Danielle Chard, Chelsi Chipps, Emmy Christopherson, Diana Cimadamore, John Clover, Alan Coffman, Mary Jo Collins, Jeffrey Colwell, Catherine Conroy, Emily Cook and brother, Megan Cook, Dee Cook-Whitlatch, Michelle Cornelius, **Sherrie Cotton,** Marissa Covarrubias, **Josh and Cassi Cox,** The Coylar Family, Michael Cross, **Sharon Dale,** Erika Davila, Carlos A. de Alba, Jessica de la Vara, Jess Delgado, Justin DeMartini, Mike Demopoulos, Jeremiah Dempsey, Jacob DePriest, Tim Devine, Matt Dickerson, Casey Dietz, Thea Dodge, Phillip Donnelly, Tom Donnelly, Jaime Doyle, Maria Dufault, Madison Dunn, Lindsey E., Michael Early, Kyle Edison, Chad Elliot, John Emmert, Scott Evans, Victor Evora, Miranda Michelle Felice, Joel Feria, Jennifer Fernandez, Troy and Cheyanne Field, Rob Fitzpatrick, Nicholas Fleming, Joe Flowers, Melissa Forte, Keitaro Francisco, Matthew Furstenfeld, Ben G., Robert Gainor, Curt Gale, **Jason Gall,** Ryan Gall, Michele Galvez, Jon Gambill, Joshua Garces, Valerie Garren, **Sharon Gee,** Sam Gennawey, Amy Gervais, Staci Gleed, Tyler Glynn, Alec Goldberg, Jimmy Golden, Micheline Golden, Reyna Gonzalez, Jeremiah Good, Jordan Goodman, Alex Goslar, Tim Grassey, Michael Greening, Christine Griffith, Josh Grothem, Werner Grundlingh, Kimberly Gryte, Carl H., Dave H., Elaine H., Josh and Alyssa and Melody Hadeen, Michael Hadlock, Holly Haider, John Hall, Sarah Hall, The Hallak Family, Rachel Hammond, Brian Hancock, Jon Handler, Chris Hansen, Cynthia Hess, Kate Heylman, Alec Hickman, **Mari Highleyman,** Carl Hoffman, Paul Hoffman, **Milton Holecek,** Michael Hollingsworth, Ethan Holmes, Chas Howell, Cory Hughes, Robert Huntington, Bill Iadonisi, Malaine Ivy-Decker, Tara Jacob, Molly Jane, Sharise Jaso, Loren Javier, **Mike Johansen,** James Johnson, Amy Jones, Michelle June, Gordon K., Matt K., Tom K., Summer Kane, Jennifer Kanihan, Andranik Karapetian, **Mehlanie Kayra,** Ryan Kehoe, Della Kingsland, Xela Knarf, Andrew Knight, Matthew and Missy Knoll, Keri Kruger, Dalia Kuarez, Meghan Kueny-Thornburg, Jackie Kushnier, Chase L., Christine Lamar, Kimberly Lamb, Rhonda Lampitt, Ledawn Larsen, Cortney Laurence, Martin Lee, Phillip Lemon, Andrew Lepire, Tony Lepore, Annie Lin, Ronald Lindberg, Alysia Lippetti, Myrna Litt, Ryan Lizama, Lourdes Llanes, Allison Lloyd, Joe Loecsey, Amber Lopez, Brian Z. Lucas, Katherine Lugo, Sal Lugo, Thao Luong, Austin M., Christina M., Henry Macall, Heather Mackey, Hank Mahler, Maria Maki, C. Mallonee, Cori Mallonee, Dawn Maple, Jorge Mario, Jasmine Martinez, John Martinez, Juan M. Martinez Ill, Paul Martinez, Dave Marx, **Michael Mason,** Kim McClaughry, Krystle McClung, Ciara McGovern, James Mcguine, Cindy McKeown, Connor McKeown, Sylvia McNeil, Oscar Mejorado, Bill and Kari Middeke, Anthony Miele, Phoebe Mikalonis, Justine Mikhail, The Miles

Family, Dallas Millam, Randi Miller, Robert Miller, Amanda Mitton, Kotomi Miyajima, Sandy Montelongo, Robert Montiel, Christopher Morales, Jose Moran, Carlos Moreno, Rebecca Mortin, Danny Mui, The Muklewicz Family, Tom Nadzieja, Lindsey Naizer, **Bobby Naus,** Kristen Naus, Andy Neitzert, A. Nelson, Aly Nelson, Aryn Nelson, J. Nelson, Marina Nelson, Dave and Kim Ness, Jay Nicholson, Ty Nielson, Daniel Nieto, Joseph Nolan, Jen O'Bryan, Elaine Ojeda, Michael and Wendy Olayvar, Jennifer Oliphant, Gillian O'Neal, Ryan Ong, Orlando Attractions magazine, **Steve Orme,** Greg Ostravich, Jessica Outhet, Andrew P., Joey P., Monica Garcia Montero P., Sam P., Priscilla Padilla, Shawna Park, Steve Parmley, Justin Parnell, Anika Patel, Cherna Patterson, Winston Peacock, Mark Pellegrini, Brian A. Pellowski, Cheyenne Pemberton, Rob and Buffy and Anna and Julia Penttila, Jennifer Peterson, Christopher Phelan, Leslie Phillips, Eric Polk, Roger Pollard, Diana Poncini, Heather Pone, Robert Powers, Kaitlyn Pratt, Melanie Price, Alyssa Proudfoot, Carlos Quintanilla, Marv R., Louise Rafferty, BJ Ralphs, Angel Ramirez, Sal Ramirez, Brendan Ratner, Sara Reid, Caleb Richards, Leslie Richards, Linda Richards, Marv Richards, Alex Roake, Jacob Robbins, Max Roberts, Joy E. Robertson-Finley, Jeff Robinson, Jose Rodriguez, Katie Rogers, Geoff Rogos, George Rojas, Shaun Rosen, Lucas Ross, Todd Rosspencer, Jean Rowley, Julian Rucki, Jessica Ruggles, Caleb Ruiz, Richard Ruiz, **Russ Rylee,** John Salinas, Ron Salinas, Jennifer Salvatierra, Dominic Sanna, Bianca and Nathan and Isaac Santoro, Brandie Sargent, Candace and Emily and Ethan Sauter, Andy Schelb, Kaleigh Schiro, Zod Schultz, P. Schwarz, Tony "Bonz" Sciortino, Chris Scott, Kira Scott, Tim Scott, Lauren Seibert, Lisa Sentif, Khrys Sganga,

The Shank Family, Nate Sharp, Michael Shearin, Mark Sheppard, The Sherrick Family, Derek Shimozaki, Ryan Shimozaki, Heather Sievers, Zach Simes, Amy Simpson, Shannan Sinclair, Nick Skiles, Breana Nicole Smith, Rebecca Smith, Jose Solano, Christopher Solesbee, Braden Stanley, Brad Steinbrenner, Lloyd Stevens, Anastasia Stewart, Darrell St. Pierre, Taylor Stratton, Chris Strodder (author of "The Disneyland Book of Lists"), Jessica Strom, Tyler Struck, Rich Sylvester, Erin T., Mitch T., Stacy T., Donna Taing, Mark Talle, Stacy Tanaka, Pat Tee, Nikolas Tejeda, Mark Temte, Craig R. Thompson, Darin Thompson, Sheryl Thompson, Joseph Thorne, Sandy Thornton, Andrew Thorp, The Tierney Family, Tim Titus, Micaela Tracy, Mark Treiger, Amy and Donnie Triphan, The Trujillo Family, Shantelle Ullery (Instagram @disneylandtourguide), Karen Ullman (and her Storybook Land Guide), Eric Upah, Christian Urcia, **Luis Valdez,** Ryan Valle, Kim Vander Dussen, Sam Vanderspek, Jessica Van Linge, Jeff Van Ry, Aldo Velez, Evelyn Vides, Juliet Violette, Fred Vosecky, Heather W., Ron W., Brock Waidmann, Mel Waidmann III, Melvin Waidmann II, Rhonda Waidmann, William Waidmann, Barrie and Jack Waldman-Marker, Chris Walhof, Scott and Kate Walker, Matt Walsh, Yvonne Washburn, Bud Webb, Sharla Webb, Austin Weber, Angela Welliver, Carolyn Whiteford, Christopher Williams, Deb Wills, Ken Wilson, Emily Woods, Gracie Wright, Jack Wright, Laura Wright, Jeanine Yamanaka, Lynn Yaw, Justin Yert, Ava Z., and Monique Zimmer.

AND

AJ, Alan, Alex, Alexa, Alexz, Amanda, Amber, Amy, Angel, Ari, Audrey, Austin, BP, Brittany, Burley, Cathy, Celandra, Cherna, Chris, Christopher, C.J., C.K., Claire, Cole, Cori, Daniel, Danny, Dee, Derrick, Destiny, Dianna, disneyland21, DVC Cast Member, Elizabeth, Emily, Emmett, Eric, **Eric and Colleen and Julie,** ES, Evan, Hans, Hayden, Hayley, Heather, **Helen and Danny,** Imp, Informer, JC, Jen, Jessica, Jonathan, Josh, Julie, Justin, Kayleigh, Kelsey, Kendra, Kevin, Kim, Krister, Kristen and family, KS and CK, Laura, Laura and Lily, Laura and Memoree, Lea Ann, Lloyd, LMD Hidden Mickey Finders, Lori, Luke, Mari, Mark, Matt, Matt@OrlandoAttractionsMagazine, Matthew, Meg, Megan, Melissa, Michaela, Mike, M. L., Morgan, Nathan, Nicky, Nitza, Nix, Nolan, Nusy, Olivia, Peter, Pinky, Queenkoalaandme, Rachel, RaeLynn, Rhonda, **Rosemary and Neil (FindingMickey.com),** Ryan, Sam, Sandy, Sara, Sarah, Sawyer, Scott, Seeing, Serena, Shannon, Shaun, Shirlyn, Stephanie, Sylvia, **Tamera,** Taylor, Teressa, Tia, Toneto and Laura and Steph, Tracy, Ty, Wayne, **Where's Mickey (myspace.com/wheresmickey),** Xander, Ylimegirl, Zod, and Zoe.

Note: This Index includes only those rides, restaurants, shops, hotels and other places in the Disneyland Resort that harbor confirmed Hidden Mickeys. If the attraction you're looking for isn't included, Mickey isn't hiding there. Or if he is, I haven't spotted him yet.

- Steve Barrett

The following abbreviations appear in this Index:
DL - Disneyland Park
CA - Disney California Adventure Park
DD - Downtown Disney District
RH - Resort Hotel